BILLY BUDD

the extraordinary study of a "natural" man, has achieved the status of a masterpiece since its posthumous publication in 1924. It tells of the plight of young Billy who finds himself assailed by uncontrollable forces, which even an impartially administered justice cannot appease.

The Reader's Supplement to this ENRICHED CLASSICS edition appears in the center insert. It has been prepared under the supervision of an editorial committee directed by Harry Shefter, Professor of English, New York University, and author of many books used extensively for the improvement of skills in the language arts. The contributing editor for this edition was Professor Richard J. Powers, Marymount College. An introduction, written for the original edition of *Billy Budd* by Maxwell Geismar, has been incorporated into the Reader's Supplement. Grateful acknowledgment is made to the Picture Collection Division of the New York Public Library which provided much of the illustrative material.

Herman Melville

Billy Budd

WASHINGTON SQUARE PRESS
PUBLISHED BY POCKET BOOKS NEW YORK

WSP

A Washington Square Press Publication of
POCKET BOOKS, a division of Simon & Schuster, Inc.
1230 Avenue of the Americas, New York, N.Y. 10020

Text of *Billy Budd* edited by Frederic Barron Freeman
and corrected by Elizabeth Treeman, reprinted by
permission of Harvard University Press. Copyright
1948 © 1956 by Harvard University Press; copyright
© 1962 by Simon & Schuster, Inc.
Reader's Supplement copyright
© 1966, 1972 by Simon & Schuster, Inc.

ISBN: 0-671-46716-6

First Pocket Books printing June, 1972

15   14   13   12   11   10   9   8

WASHINGTON SQUARE PRESS, WSP and colophon are
registered trademarks of Simon & Schuster, Inc.

Printed in the U.S.A.

I

IN THE TIME before steamships, or then more frequently than now, a stroller along the docks of any considerable seaport would occasionally have his attention arrested by a group of bronzed mariners, man-of-war's men or merchant-sailors in holiday attire ashore on liberty. In certain instances they would flank, or, like a bodyguard quite surround some superior figure of their own class, moving along with them like Aldebaran[1] among the lesser lights of his constellation. That signal object was the "Handsome Sailor" of the less prosaic time alike of the military and merchant navies. With no perceptible trace of the vainglorious about him, rather with the off-hand unaffectedness of natural regality, he seemed to accept the spontaneous homage of his shipmates. A somewhat remarkable instance recurs to me. In Liverpool, now half a century ago I saw under the shadow of the great dingy street-wall of Prince's Dock (an obstruction long since removed) a common sailor, so intensely black that he must needs have been a native African of the unadulterate blood of Ham.[2] A symmetric figure much above the average height. The two ends of a gay silk handkerchief thrown loose about the neck danced upon the displayed ebony of his chest; in his ears were big hoops of gold, and a Scotch Highland bonnet with a tartan band set off his shapely head.

It was a hot noon in July; and his face, lustrous with perspiration, beamed with barbaric good humor. In jovial sallies right and left, his white teeth flashing into view, he rollicked

---

1 This large red star was regarded by the ancients as the "eye" of the Bull, the constellation Taurus.

2 In popular superstition, the Negroes, because Noah laid the curse of servitude upon the descendants of his youngest son, Ham, who mocked him; *cf.* Genesis ix: 22–25.

along, the center of a company of his shipmates. These were made up of such an assortment of tribes and complexions as would have well fitted them to be marched up by Anacharsis Cloots[3] before the bar of the first French Assembly as representatives of the human race. At each spontaneous tribute rendered by the wayfarers to this black pagod of a fellow— the tribute of a pause and stare, and less frequent an exclamation—the motley retinue showed that they took that sort of pride in the evoker of it which the Assyrian priests doubtless showed for their grand sculptured bull when the faithful prostrated themselves.

To return.

If in some cases a bit of a nautical Murat[4] in setting forth his person ashore, the handsome sailor of the period in question evinced nothing of the dandified Billy-be-Damn, an amusing character all but extinct now, but occasionally to be encountered, and in a form yet more amusing than the original, at the tiller of the boats on the tempestuous Erie Canal or, more likely, vaporing in the groggeries along the towpath. Invariably a proficient in his perilous calling, he was also more or less of a mighty boxer or wrestler. It was strength and beauty. Tales of his prowess were recited. Ashore he was the champion; afloat the spokesman; on every suitable occasion always foremost. Close-reefing topsails in a gale, there he was, astride the weather yardarm end, foot in the Flemish horse as "stirrup," both hands tugging at the "earring" as at a bridle, in very much the attitude of young Alexander curbing the fiery Bucephalus.[5] A superb figure, tossed up as by the horns of Taurus against the thunderous sky, cheerily hallooing to the strenuous file along the spar.

The moral nature was seldom out of keeping with the physical make. Indeed, except as toned by the former, the

---

3 Carlyle, in his *French Revolution* (1837), popularized Cloots's escapade, as here described, by which he claimed the democratic privileges of the Assembly for this group representing various countries and stations.

4 Joachim Murat (1767?–1815); French military adventurer, and conspirator with Napoleon. As King of Naples he was called "the Dandy King" for his foppishness.

5 The famous war horse of Alexander the Great (356–323 B.C.)

comeliness and power, always attractive in masculine conjunction, hardly could have drawn the sort of honest homage the Handsome Sailor in some examples received from his less gifted associates.

Such a cynosure, at least in aspect, and something such too in nature, though with important variations made apparent as the story proceeds, was welkin-eyed Billy Budd, or Baby Budd as more familiarly under circumstances hereafter to be given he at last came to be called, aged twenty-one, a foretopman of the British fleet toward the close of the last decade of the eighteenth century. It was not very long prior to the time of the narration that follows that he had entered the King's service, having been impressed[6] on the Narrow Seas from a homeward-bound English merchantman into a seventy-four[8] outward-bound, H.M.S. *Indomitable;* which ship, as was not unusual in those hurried days having been obliged to put to sea short of her proper complement of men. Plump upon Billy at first sight in the gangway the boarding officer Lieutenant Ratcliffe pounced, even before the merchantman's crew was formally mustered on the quarterdeck for his deliberate inspection. And him only he elected. For whether it was because the other men when ranged before him showed to ill advantage after Billy, or whether he had some scruples in view of the merchantman being rather shorthanded, however it might be, the officer contented himself with his first spontaneous choice. To the surprise of the ship's company, though much to the lieutenant's satisfaction Billy made no demur. But, indeed, any demur would have been as idle as the protest of a goldfinch popped into a cage.

Noting this uncomplaining acquiescence, all but cheerful one might say, the shipmates turned a surprised glance of silent reproach at the sailor. The shipmaster was one of those worthy mortals found in every vocation even the humbler ones—the sort of person whom everybody agrees in calling

---

6 Laws covering British naval recruitment then permitted commanders to complete their crews by forcing, or "impressing," merchant sailors, on land or sea, into service.

7 *I.e.*, a ship carrying seventy-four guns.

"a respectable man." And—nor so strange to report as it may appear to be—though a ploughman of the troubled waters, life-long contending with the intractable elements, there was nothing this honest soul at heart loved better than simple peace and quiet. For the rest, he was fifty or thereabouts, a little inclined to corpulence, a prepossessing face, unwhiskered, and of an agreeable color—a rather full face, humanely intelligent in expression. On a fair day with a fair wind and all going well, a certain musical chime in his voice seemed to be the veritable unobstructed outcome of the innermost man. He had much prudence, much conscientiousness, and there were occasions when these virtues were the cause of overmuch disquietude in him. On a passage, so long as his craft was in any proximity to land, no sleep for Captain Graveling. He took to heart those serious responsibilities not so heavily borne by some shipmasters.

Now while Billy Budd was down in the forecastle getting his kit together, the *Indomitable's* lieutenant, burly and bluff, nowise disconcerted by Captain Graveling's omitting to proffer the customary hospitalities on an occasion so unwelcome to him, an omission simply caused by preoccupation of thought, unceremoniously invited himself into the cabin, and also to a flask from the spirit locker, a receptacle which his experienced eye instantly discovered. In fact he was one of those sea dogs in whom all the hardship and peril of naval life in the great prolonged wars of his time never impaired the natural instinct for sensuous enjoyment. His duty he always faithfully did; but duty is sometimes a dry obligation, and he was for irrigating its aridity, whensoever possible, with a fertilizing decoction of strong waters. For the cabin's proprietor there was nothing left but to play the part of the enforced host with whatever grace and alacrity were practicable. As necessary adjuncts to the flask, he silently placed tumbler and water jug before the irrepressible guest. But excusing himself from partaking just then, he dismally watched the unembarrassed officer deliberately diluting his grog a little, then tossing it off in three swallows, pushing the empty tumbler away, yet not so far as to be beyond easy reach, at the same time settling himself in his seat and smacking his lips with high satisfaction, looking straight at the host.

These proceedings over, the master broke the silence; and there lurked a rueful reproach in the tone of his voice; "Lieutenant, you are going to take my best man from me, the jewel of 'em."

"Yes, I know," rejoined the other, immediately drawing back the tumbler preliminary to a replenishing; "Yes, I know. Sorry."

"Beg pardon, but you don't understand, Lieutenant. See here now. Before I shipped that young fellow, my forecastle was a rat-pit of quarrels. It was black times, I tell you, aboard the *'Rights'* here. I was worried to that degree my pipe had no comfort for me. But Billy came; and it was like a Catholic priest striking peace in an Irish shindy. Not that he preached to them or did anything in particular; but a virtue went out of him, sugaring the sour ones. They took to him like hornets to treacle; all but the buffer of the gang, the big shaggy chap with the fire-red whiskers. He indeed out of envy, perhaps, of the newcomer, and thinking such a 'sweet and pleasant fellow,' as he mockingly designated him to the others, could hardly have the spirit of a gamecock, must needs bestir himself in trying to get up an ugly row with him. Billy forebore with him and reasoned with him in a pleasant way—he is something like myself, Lieutenant, to whom aught like a quarrel is hateful—but nothing served. So, in the second dog-watch one day the Red Whiskers in presence of the others, under the pretence of showing Billy just whence a sirloin steak was cut—for the fellow had once been a butcher—insultingly gave him a dig under the ribs. Quick as lightning Billy let fly his arm. I dare say he never meant to do quite as much as he did, but anyhow he gave the burly fool a terrible drubbing. It took about half a minute, I should think. And, lord bless you, the lubber was astonished at the celerity. And will you believe it, Lieutenant, the Red Whiskers now really loves Billy—loves him, or is the biggest hypocrite that ever I heard of. But they all love him. Some of 'em do his washing, darn his old trousers for him; the carpenter is at odd times making a pretty little chest of drawers for him. Anybody will do anything for Billy Budd; and it's the happy family here. But now, Lieutenant, if that young fellow goes —I know how it will be aboard the '*Rights.*' Not again very soon shall I, coming up from dinner, lean over the capstan smoking a quiet pipe—no, not very soon again, I think. Ay, Lieutenant, you are going to take away the jewel of 'em; you are going to take away my peacemaker!" And with that the good soul had really some ado in checking a rising sob.

"Well," said the officer who had listened with amused interest to all this, and was now waxing merry with his tipple; "Well, blessed are the peacemakers especially the fighting peacemakers! And such are the seventy-four beauties some of which you see poking their noses out of the portholes of yonder warship lying-to for me" pointing through the cabin window at the *Indomitable.* "But courage! don't look so downhearted, man. Why, I pledge you in advance the royal approbation. Rest assured that His Majesty will be delighted to know that in a time when his hardtack is not sought for by sailors with such avidity as should be; a time also when some shipmasters privily resent the borrowing from them a tar or two for the service; His Majesty, I say, will be delighted to learn that one shipmaster at least cheerfully surrenders to the King, the flower of his flock, a sailor who with equal loyalty makes no dissent— But where's my beauty? Ah," looking through the cabin's open door, "here he comes; and, by Jove —lugging along his chest—Apollo with his portmanteau!— My man," stepping out to him, "you can't take that big box aboard a warship. The boxes there are mostly shot-boxes. Put your duds in a bag, lad. Boot and saddle for the cavalryman, bag and hammock for the man-of-war's man."

The transfer from chest to bag was made. And, after seeing his man into the cutter and then following him down, the lieutenant pushed off from the *Rights-of-Man.* That was the merchant-ship's name; though by her master and crew abbreviated in sailor fashion into *The Rights.* The hardheaded Dundee owner was a staunch admirer of Thomas Paine whose book in rejoinder to Burke's arraignment of the French

Revolution had then been published for some time and had gone everywhere. In christening his vessel after the title of Paine's volume the man of Dundee was something like his contemporary shipowner, Stephen Girard[8] of Philadelphia, whose sympathies, alike with his native land and its liberal philosophers, he evinced by naming his ships after Voltaire, Diderot, and so forth.

But now, when the boat swept under the merchantman's stern and officer and oarsmen were noting—some bitterly and others with a grin—the name emblazoned there; just then it was that the new recruit jumped up from the bow where the coxswain had directed him to sit, and waving his hat to his silent shipmates sorrowfully looking over at him from the taffrail, bade the lads a genial good-by. Then, making a salutation as to the ship herself, "And good-by to you too, old *Rights of Man*."

"Down, sir!" roared the lieutenant, instantly assuming all the rigor of his rank, though with difficulty repressing a smile.

To be sure, Billy's action was a terrible breach of naval decorum. But in that decorum he had never been instructed; in consideration of which the lieutenant would hardly have been so energetic in reproof but for the concluding farewell to the ship. This he rather took as meant to convey a covert sally on the new recruit's part, a sly slur at impressment in general, and that of himself in especial. And yet, more likely, if satire it was in effect, it was hardly so by intention, for Billy though happily endowed with the gayety of high health, youth, and a free heart, was yet by no means of a satirical turn. The will to it and the sinister dexterity were alike wanting. To deal in double meanings and insinuation of any sort was quite foreign to his nature.

As to his enforced enlistment, that he seemed to take pretty much as he was wont to take any vicissitude of weather. Like the animals, though no philosopher, he was, without knowing it, practically a fatalist. And, it may be that he rather liked

8 Girard (1750–1831), the great Philadelphia merchant and banker, remained in his native France until he was twenty-seven, and read widely among the liberal authors of that period.

this adventurous turn in his affairs, which promised an opening into novel scenes and martial excitements.

Aboard the *Indomitable* our merchant-sailor was forthwith rated as an able seaman and assigned to the starboard watch of the foretop. He was soon at home in the service, not at all disliked for his unpretentious good looks and a sort of genial happy-go-lucky air. No merrier man in his mess: in marked contrast to certain other individuals included like himself among the impressed portion of the ship's company; for these when not actively employed were sometimes, and more particularly in the last dogwatch when the drawing near of twilight induced revery, apt to fall into a saddish mood which in some partook of sullenness. But they were not so young as our foretopman, and no few of them must have known a hearth of some sort, others may have had wives and children left, too probably, in uncertain circumstances, and hardly any but must have had acknowledged kith and kin, while for Billy, as will shortly be seen, his entire family was practically invested in himself.

II

THOUGH OUR NEW-MADE foretopman was well received in the top and on the gundecks, hardly here was he that cynosure he had previously been among those minor ship's companies of the merchant marine, with which companies only had he hitherto consorted.

He was young; and despite his all but fully developed frame in aspect looked even younger than he really was, owing to a lingering adolescent expression in the as yet smooth face all but feminine in purity of natural complexion but where, thanks to his seagoing, the lily was quite suppressed and the rose had some ado visibly to flush through the tan.

To one essentially such a novice in the complexities of factitious life, the abrupt transition from his former and simpler sphere to the ampler and more knowing world of a great warship; this might well have abashed him had there

been any conceit or vanity in his composition. Among her
miscellaneous multitude, the *Indomitable* mustered several individuals who however inferior in grade were of no common
natural stamp, sailors more signally susceptive of that air
which continuous martial discipline and repeated presence in
battle can in some degree impart even to the average man.
As the *handsome sailor* Billy Budd's position aboard the
seventy-four was something analogous to that of a rustic
beauty transplanted from the provinces and brought into
competition with the highborn dames of the court. But this
change of circumstances he scarce noted. As little did he
observe that something about him provoked an ambiguous
smile in one or two harder faces among the blue-jackets.
Nor less unaware was he of the peculiar favorable effect his
person and demeanor had upon the more intelligent gentlemen of the quarterdeck. Nor could this well have been otherwise. Cast in a mold peculiar to the finest physical examples
of those Englishmen in whom the Saxon strain would seem
not at all to partake of any Norman or other admixture, he
showed in fact that humane look of reposeful good nature
which the Greek sculptor in some instances gave to his heroic
strong man, Hercules. But this again was subtly modified
by another and pervasive quality. The ear, small and shapely,
the arch of the foot, the curve in mouth and nostril, even
the indurated hand dyed to the orange-tawny of the toucan's
bill, a hand telling alike of the halyards and tar bucket; but,
above all, something in the mobile expression, and every
chance attitude and movement, something suggestive of a
mother eminently favored by Love and the Graces; all this
strangely indicated a lineage in direct contradiction to his
lot. The mysteriousness here, became less mysterious through
a matter-of-fact elicited when Billy at the capstan was being
formally mustered into the service. Asked by the officer, a
small brisk little gentleman as it chanced among other questions, his place of birth, he replied, "Please, sir, I don't
know."

"Don't know where you were born?— Who was your
father?"

"God knows, sir."

Struck by the straightforward simplicity of these replies, the officer next asked "Do you know anything about your beginning?"

"No, sir. But I have heard that I was found in a pretty silk-lined basket hanging one morning from the knocker of a good man's door in Bristol."

"*Found* say you? Well," throwing back his head and looking up and down the new recruit; "Well, it turns out to have been a pretty good find. Hope they'll find some more like you, my man; the fleet sadly needs them."

Yes, Billy Budd was a foundling, a presumable bye-blow,[9] and, evidently, no ignoble one. Noble descent was as evident in him as in a blood horse.

For the rest, with little or no sharpness of faculty or any trace of the wisdom of the serpent, nor yet quite a dove, he possessed that kind and degree of intelligence going along with the unconventional rectitude of a sound human creature, one to whom not yet has been proffered the questionable apple of knowledge. He was illiterate; he could not read, but he could sing, and like the illiterate nightingale was sometimes the composer of his own song.

Of self-consciousness he seemed to have little or none, or about as much as we may reasonably impute to a dog of Saint Bernard's breed.

Habitually living with the elements and knowing little more of the land than as a beach, or, rather, that portion of the terraqueous globe providentially set apart for dance-houses' doxies and tapsters, in short what sailors call a "fiddlers' green," his simple nature remained unsophisticated by those moral obliquities which are not in every case incompatible with that manufacturable thing known as respectability. But are sailors, frequenters of "fiddlers' greens," without vices? No; but less often than with landsmen do their vices, so called, partake of crookedness of heart, seeming less to proceed from viciousness than exuberance of vitality after long constraint;

---

9 Usually, "by-blow"—an illegitimate child.

frank manifestations in accordance with natural law. By his original constitution aided by the co-operating influences of his lot, Billy in many respects was little more than a sort of upright barbarian, much such perhaps as Adam presumably might have been ere the urbane serpent wriggled himself into his company.

And here be it submitted that apparently going to corroborate the doctrine of man's fall, a doctrine now popularly ignored, it is observable that where certain virtues pristine and unadulterate peculiarly characterize anybody in the external uniform of civilization, they will upon scrutiny seem not to be derived from custom or convention, but rather to be out of keeping with these, as if indeed exceptionally transmitted from a period prior to Cain's city and citified man. The character marked by such qualities has to an unvitiated taste an untampered-with flavor like that of berries, while the man thoroughly civilized even in a fair specimen of the breed has to the same moral palate a questionable smack as of a compounded wine. To any stray inheritor of these primitive qualities found, like Caspar Hauser,[1] wandering dazed in any Christian capital of our time the good-natured poet's famous invocation, near two thousand years ago, of the good rustic out of his latitude in the Rome of the Caesars, still appropriately holds:

> "Honest and poor, faithful in word and thought
>   What has thee, Fabian, to the city brought."[2]

Though our Handsome Sailor had as much of masculine beauty as one can expect anywhere to see; nevertheless, like the beautiful woman in one of Hawthorne's minor tales,[3] there was just one thing amiss in him. No visible blemish indeed, as with the lady; no, but an occasional liability to a vocal defect.

---

1 Kaspar Hauser (1812?–1833) mysteriously appeared in 1828 in Nuremberg, Germany. Popularly imagined to be of noble birth, he aroused international attention, and was mysteriously assassinated.

2 Martial, *Epigrams,* Book IV, 5.

3 Apparently "The Birthmark."

Though in the hour of elemental uproar or peril, he was everything that a sailor should be, yet under sudden provocation of strong heart-feeling his voice otherwise singularly musical, as if expressive of the harmony within, was apt to develop an organic hesitancy, in fact more or less of a stutter or even worse. In this particular Billy was a striking instance that the arch interferer, the envious marplot of Eden still has more or less to do with every human consignment to this planet of earth. In every case, one way or another he is sure to slip in his little card, as much as to remind us—I too have a hand here.

The avowal of such an imperfection in the Handsome Sailor should be evidence not alone that he is not presented as a conventional hero, but also that the story in which he is the main figure is no romance.

III

AT THE TIME of Billy Budd's arbitrary enlistment into the *Indomitable* that ship was on her way to join the Mediterranean fleet. No long time elapsed before the junction was effected. As one of that fleet the seventy-four participated in its movements, though at times on account of her superior sailing qualities, in the absence of frigates, dispatched on separate duty as a scout and at times on less temporary service. But with all this the story has little concernment, restricted as it is to the inner life of one particular ship and the career of an individual sailor.

It was the summer of 1797. In the April of that year had occurred the commotion at Spithead followed in May by a second and yet more serious outbreak in the fleet at the Nore. The latter is known, and without exaggeration in the epithet, as the Great Mutiny. It was indeed a demonstration more menacing to England than the contemporary manifestoes and conquering and proselyting armies of the French Directory.

To the British Empire the Nore Mutiny was what a strike in the fire brigade would be to London threatened by general

arson. In a crisis when the kingdom might well have anticipated the famous signal that some years later published along
the naval line of battle what it was that upon occasion England expected of Englishmen;[4] *that* was the time when at the
mastheads of the three-deckers and seventy-fours moored in
her own roadstead—a fleet, the right arm of a power then
all but the sole free conservative one of the Old World, the
blue-jackets, to be numbered by thousands, ran up with huzzas
the British colors with the union and cross wiped out; by that
cancellation transmuting the flag of founded law and freedom
defined, into the enemy's red meteor of unbridled and un-
bounded revolt. Reasonable discontent growing out of practical grievances in the fleet had been ignited into irrational
combustion as by live cinders blown across the Channel from
France in flames.

The event converted into irony for a time those spirited
strains of Dibdin[5]—as a songwriter no means auxiliary to the
English government at the European conjuncture—strains cele-
brating, among other things, the patriotic devotion of the
British tar:

"And as for my life, 'tis the King's!"

Such an episode in the island's grand naval story her naval
historians naturally abridge; one of them (G. P. R. James)[6]
candidly acknowledging that fain would he pass it over did
not "impartiality forbid fastidiousness." And yet his mention
is less a narration than a reference, having to do hardly at all
with details. Nor are these readily to be found in the libraries.
Like some other events in every age befalling states everywhere including America the Great Mutiny was of such
character that national pride along with views of policy

---

4 In 1805, in the naval battle against the French and Spanish off Trafalgar,
where he was killed, Admiral Nelson ran up the famous signal "England expects every man to do his duty."

5 Charles Dibdin (1745–1814) was an English dramatist, but his enduring
fame rests on his sailor songs and chanteys.

6 G. P. R. James (1799–1860), a very popular and prolific British novelist.

would fain shade it off into the historical background. Such events can not be ignored, but there is a considerate way of historically treating them. If a well-constituted individual refrains from blazoning aught amiss or calamitous in his family; a nation in the like circumstance may without reproach be equally discreet.

Though after parleyings between government and the ringleaders, and concessions by the former as to some glaring abuses, the first uprising—that at Spithead—with difficulty was put down, or matters for the time pacified; yet at the Nore the unforeseen renewal of insurrection on a yet larger scale, and emphasized in the conferences that ensued by demands deemed by the authorities not only inadmissible but aggressively insolent, indicated—if the red flag did not sufficiently do so—what was the spirit animating the men. Final suppression, however, there was; but only made possible perhaps by the unswerving loyalty of the marine corps and voluntary resumption of loyalty among influential sections of the crews.

To some extent the Nore Mutiny may be regarded as analogous to the distempering irruption of contagious fever in a frame constitutionally sound, and which anon throws it off.

At all events, of these thousands of mutineers were some of the tars who not so very long afterwards—whether wholly prompted thereto by patriotism, or pugnacious instinct, or by both,—helped to win a coronet for Nelson at the Nile,[7] and the naval crown of crowns for him at Trafalgar. To the mutineers those battles and especially Trafalgar were a plenary absolution and a grand one: for all that goes to make up scenic naval display, heroic magnificence in arms, those battles especially Trafalgar stand unmatched in human annals.

---

7 For his victory at the Nile (1798), Nelson was made a baron; later he became a viscount.

IV

Concerning "The greatest sailor since the world began." Tennyson[8]

IN THIS MATTER of writing, resolve as one may to keep to the main road, some by-paths have an enticement not readily to be withstood. I am going to err into such a by-path. If the reader will keep me company I shall be glad. At the least we can promise ourselves that pleasure which is wickedly said to be in sinning, for a literary sin the divergence will be.

Very likely it is no new remark that the inventions of our time have at last brought about a change in sea warfare in degree corresponding to the revolution in all warfare effected by the original introduction from China into Europe of gunpowder. The first European firearm, a clumsy contrivance, was, as well known, scouted by no few of the knights as a base implement, good enough peradventure for weavers too craven to stand up crossing steel with steel in frank fight. But as ashore knightly valor though shorn of its blazonry did not cease with the knights, neither on the seas though nowadays in encounters there a certain kind of displayed gallantry be fallen out of date as hardly applicable under changed circumstances, did the nobler qualities of such naval magnates as Don John of Austria, Doria, Van Tromp, Jean Bart, the long line of British admirals and the American Decaturs of 1812 become obsolete with their wooden walls.[9]

---

8 The line, which is line 7 in Tennyson's "Ode on the Death of the Duke of Wellington" (1852), reads: "The greatest sailor since our world began."

9 All famous "iron admirals" of the wooden ships. Don John of Austria commanded the fleet of the Holy League in the defeat of the Turks at Lepanto (1571); Andrea Doria (1468–1560), Genoese admiral, was the "Liberator of Genoa" from the Turks; Maarten Tromp (1597–1653) commanded the Dutch fleets in struggles for independence from Spain, Portugal, and Britain; Jean Bart, famous French soldier of fortune, commanded privateers against the Dutch (1686–1697); and the American naval hero Stephen Decatur was renowned for daring exploits against the Tripoli pirates (1803–1804) and for victories over British ships in the War of 1812.

Nevertheless, to anybody who can hold the present at its worth without being inappreciative of the past, it may be forgiven, if to such a one of the solitary old hulk at Portsmouth, Nelson's *Victory*, seems to float there, not alone as the decaying monument of a fame incorruptible, but also as a poetic reproach, softened by its picturesqueness, to the *Monitors*[1] and yet mightier hulls of the European ironclads. And this not altogether because such craft are unsightly, unavoidably lacking the symmetry and grand lines of the old battleships, but equally for other reasons.

There are some, perhaps, who while not altogether inaccessible to that poetic reproach just alluded to, may yet on behalf of the new order, be disposed to parry it; and this to the extent of iconoclasm, if need be. For example, prompted by the sight of the star inserted in the *Victory's* quarterdeck designating the spot where the great sailor fell, these martial utilitarians may suggest considerations implying that Nelson's ornate publication of his person in battle was not only unnecessary, but not military, nay, savored of foolhardiness and vanity. They may add, too, that at Trafalgar it was in effect nothing less than a challenge to death; and death came; and that but for his bravado the victorious Admiral might possibly have survived the battle, and so, instead of having his sagacious dying injunctions overruled by his immediate successor in command he himself when the contest was decided might have brought his shattered fleet to anchor, a proceeding which might have averted the deplorable loss of life by shipwreck in the elemental tempest that followed the martial one.

Well, should we set aside the more disputable point whether for various reasons it was possible to anchor the fleet, then plausibly enough the Benthamites[2] of war may urge the above.

But the *might-have-been* is but boggy ground to build on.

---

1 During the Civil War, the *Monitor's* defeat of the southern *Merrimac* at Hampton Roads (March, 1862) ended the first engagement between ironclad ships.

2 Jeremy Bentham (1748–1832), British jurist and utilitarian philosopher, in *Principles of Morals and Legislation* (1789) propounded his famous dictum that "the greatest happiness of the greatest number is the foundation of morals and legislation."

And, certainly, in foresight as to the larger issue of an encounter, and anxious preparations for it—buoying the deadly way and mapping it out, as at Copenhagen[3]—few commanders have been so painstakingly circumspect as this same reckless declarer of his person in fight.

Personal prudence even when dictated by quite other than selfish considerations surely is no special virtue in a military man; while an excessive love of glory, impassioning a less burning impulse, the honest sense of duty, is the first. If the name *Wellington* is not so much of a trumpet to the blood as the simpler name *Nelson*, the reason for this may perhaps be inferred from the above. Alfred[4] in his funeral ode on the victor of Waterloo ventures not to call him the greatest soldier of all time, though in the same ode he invokes Nelson as "the greatest sailor since the world began."

At Trafalgar Nelson on the brink of opening the fight sat down and wrote his last brief will and testament. If under the presentiment of the most magnificent of all victories to be crowned by his own glorious death, a sort of priestly motive led him to dress his person in the jeweled vouchers of his own shining deeds; if thus to have adorned himself for the altar and the sacrifice were indeed vainglory, then affectation and fustian is each more heroic line in the great epics and dramas, since in such lines the poet but embodies in verse those exaltations of sentiment that a nature like Nelson, the opportunity being given, vitalizes into acts.

V

YES, THE OUTBREAK at the Nore was put down. But not every grievance was redressed. If the contractors, for example, were no longer permitted to ply some practices peculiar to their tribe everywhere, such as providing shoddy cloth, rations not sound, or false in the measure, not the less impressment, for one thing, went on. By custom sanctioned for centuries, and

---

3 Nelson's siege of Copenhagen (1801) became a famous example of strategy.

4 *I.e.*, Tennyson; *cf.* epigraph to this chapter.

judicially maintained by a lord chancellor as late as Mansfield,[5] that mode of manning the fleet, a mode now fallen into a sort of abeyance but never formally renounced, it was not practicable to give up in those years. Its abrogation would have crippled the indispensable fleet, one wholly under canvas, no steam power, its innumerable sails and thousands of cannon, everything in short, worked by muscle alone; a fleet the more insatiate in demand for men, because then multiplying its ships of all grades against contingencies present and to come of the convulsed Continent.

Discontent foreran the two mutinies, and more or less it lurkingly survived them. Hence it was not unreasonable to apprehend some return of trouble sporadic or general. One instance of such apprehensions: In the same year with this story, Nelson, then Vice Admiral Sir Horatio, being with the fleet off the Spanish coast, was directed by the admiral in command to shift his pennant from the *Captain* to the *Theseus;* and for this reason: that the latter ship having newly arrived on the station from home where it had taken part in the Great Mutiny, danger was apprehended from the temper of the men; and it was thought that an officer like Nelson was the one, not indeed to terrorize the crew into base subjection, but to win them, by force of his mere presence back to an allegiance if not as enthusiastic as his own, yet as true. So it was that for a time on more than one quarterdeck anxiety did exist. At sea precautionary vigilance was strained against relapse. At short notice an engagement might come on. When it did, the lieutenants assigned to batteries felt it incumbent on them, in some instances, to stand with drawn swords behind the men working the guns.

VI

BUT ON BOARD the seventy-four in which Billy now swung his hammock, very little in the manner of the men and nothing obvious in the demeanor of the officers would have suggested

---

5 William Murray, Baron Mansfield, British parliamentarian, became lord chief justice in 1756, and was later a cabinet minister (1773–1788).

to an ordinary observer that the Great Mutiny was a recent event. In their general bearing and conduct the commissioned officers of a warship naturally take their tone from the commander, that is if he have that ascendancy of character that ought to be his.

Captain the Honorable Edward Fairfax Vere, to give his full title, was a bachelor of forty or thereabouts, a sailor of distinction even in a time prolific of renowned seamen. Though allied to the higher nobility his advancement had not been altogether owing to influences connected with that circumstance. He had seen much service, been in various engagements, always acquitting himself as an officer mindful of the welfare of his men, but never tolerating an infraction of discipline; thoroughly versed in the science of his profession, and intrepid to the verge of temerity, though never injudiciously so. For his gallantry in the West Indian waters as flag-lieutenant under Rodney in that admiral's crowning victory over De Grasse,[6] he was made a post-captain.

Ashore in the garb of a civilian scarce anyone would have taken him for a sailor, more especially that he never garnished unprofessional talk with nautical terms, and grave in his bearing, evinced little appreciation of mere humor. It was not out of keeping with these traits that on a passage when nothing demanded his paramount action, he was the most undemonstrative of men. Any landsman observing this gentleman not conspicuous by his stature and wearing no pronounced insignia, emerging from his cabin to the open deck, and noting the silent deference of the officers retiring to leeward, might have taken him for the King's guest, a civilian aboard the King's-ship, some highly honorable discreet envoy on his way to an important post. But in fact this unobtrusiveness of demeanor may have proceeded from a certain unaffected modesty of manhood sometimes accompanying a resolute nature, a modesty evinced at all times not calling for

6 The British admiral George Brydges, Baron Rodney (1719–1792) defeated the French admiral De Grasse in a naval engagement off Dominica, in the Leewards, in 1782.

pronounced action, and which shown in any rank of life suggests a virtue aristocratic in kind.

As with some others engaged in various departments of the world's more heroic activities, Captain Vere though practical enough upon occasion would at times betray a certain dreaminess of mood. Standing alone on the weather side of the quarterdeck, one hand holding by the rigging he would absently gaze off at the blank sea. At the presentation to him then of some minor matter interrupting the current of his thoughts he would show more or less irascibility; but instantly he would control it.

In the navy he was popularly known by the appellation—Starry Vere. How such a designation happened to fall upon one who whatever his sturdy qualities was without any brilliant ones was in this wise: A favorite kinsman, Lord Denton, a freehearted fellow, had been the first to meet and congratulate him upon his return to England from his West Indian cruise; and but the day previous turning over a copy of Andrew Marvell's poems had lighted, not for the first time however, upon the lines entitled *Appleton House,* the name of one of the seats of their common ancestor, a hero in the German wars of the seventeenth century, in which poem occur the lines,

> "This 'tis to have been from the first
> In a domestic heaven nursed,
> Under the discipline severe
> Of Fairfax and the starry Vere."

And so, upon embracing his cousin fresh from Rodney's great victory wherein he had played so gallant a part, brimming over with just family pride in the sailor of their house, he exuberantly exclaimed, "Give ye joy, Ed; give ye joy, my starry Vere!" This got currency, and the novel prefix serving in familiar parlance readily to distinguish the *Indomitable's* captain from another Vere his senior, a distant relative an officer of like rank in the navy, it remained permanently attached to the surname.

VII

IN VIEW OF the part that the commander of the *Indomitable* plays in scenes shortly to follow, it may be well to fill out that sketch of him outlined in the previous chapter.

Aside from his qualities as a sea officer Captain Vere was an exceptional character. Unlike no few of England's renowned sailors, long and arduous service with signal devotion to it, had not resulted in absorbing and *salting* the entire man. He had a marked leaning toward everything intellectual. He loved books, never going to sea without a newly replenished library, compact but of the best. The isolated leisure, in some cases so wearisome, falling at intervals to commanders even during a war cruise, never was tedious to Captain Vere. With nothing of that literary taste which less heeds the thing conveyed than the vehicle, his bias was toward those books to which every serious mind of superior order occupying any active post of authority in the world, naturally inclines: books treating of actual men and events no matter of what era—history, biography and unconventional writers, who, free from cant and convention, like Montaigne, honestly and in the spirit of common sense philosophize upon realities.

In this line of reading he found confirmation of his own more reasoned thoughts—confirmation which he had vainly sought in social converse, so that as touching most fundamental topics, there had got to be established in him some positive convictions, which he fore-felt would abide in him essentially unmodified so long as his intelligent part remained unimpaired. In view of the troubled period in which his lot was cast this was well for him. His settled convictions were as a dyke against those invading waters of novel opinion social political and otherwise, which carried away as in a torrent no few minds in those days, minds by nature not inferior to his own. While other members of that aristocracy to which by birth he belonged were incensed at the innovators mainly because their theories were inimical to the privileged classes, not alone Captain Vere disinterestedly opposed them because they seemed to him incapable of embodiment in lasting institutions, but at war with the peace of the world and the true welfare of mankind.

With minds less stored than his and less earnest, some officers of his rank, with whom at times he would necessarily consort, found him lacking in the companionable quality, a dry and bookish gentleman as they deemed. Upon any chance withdrawal from their company one would be apt to say to another, something like this: "Vere is a noble fellow, Starry Vere. Spite the gazettes, Sir Horatio" meaning him with the lord title[7] "is at bottom scarce a better seaman or fighter. But between you and me now don't you think there is a queer streak of the pedantic running through him? Yes, like the King's yarn in a coil of navy rope?"

Some apparent ground there was for this sort of confidential criticism; since not only did the captain's discourse never fall into the jocosely familiar, but in illustrating of any point touching the stirring personages and events of the time he would be as apt to cite some historic character or incident of antiquity as that he would cite from the moderns. He seemed unmindful of the circumstance that to his bluff company such remote allusions however pertinent they might really be were altogether alien to men whose reading was mainly confined to the journals. But considerateness in such matters is not easy to natures constituted like Captain Vere's. Their honesty prescribes to them directness, sometimes far-reaching like that of a migratory fowl that in its flight never heeds when it crosses a frontier.

VIII

THE LIEUTENANTS and other commissioned gentlemen forming Captain Vere's staff it is not necessary here to particularize, nor needs it to make any mention of any of the warrant-officers. But among the petty-officers was one who having much to do with the story, may as well be forthwith intro-

---

7 *I.e.*, Admiral Horatio Nelson, a viscount.

duced. His portrait I essay, but shall never hit it. This was John Claggart, the master-at-arms. But that sea title may to landsmen seem somewhat equivocal. Originally doubtless that petty-officer's function was the instruction of the men in the use of arms, sword or cutlas. But very long ago, owing to the advance in gunnery making hand-to-hand encounters less frequent and giving to niter and sulphur the pre-eminence over steel, that function ceased; the master-at-arms of a great warship becoming a sort of chief of police charged among other matters with the duty of preserving order on the populous lower gundecks.

Claggart was a man about five and thirty, somewhat spare and tall, yet of no ill figure upon the whole. His hand was too small and shapely to have been accustomed to hard toil. The face was a notable one; the features all except the chin cleanly cut as those on a Greek medallion; yet the chin, beardless as Tecumseh's,[8] had something of strange protuberant heaviness in its make that recalled the prints of the Rev. Dr. Titus Oates, the historic deponent with the clerical drawl in the time of Charles II and the fraud of the alleged Popish Plot.[9] It served Claggart in his office that his eye could cast a tutoring glance. His brow was of the sort phrenologically associated with more than average intellect; silken jet curls partly clustering over it, making a foil to the pallor below, a pallor tinged with a faint shade of amber akin to the hue of time-tinted marbles of old. This complexion, singularly contrasting with the red or deeply bronzed visages of the sailors, and in part the result of his official seclusion from the sunlight, though it was not exactly displeasing, nevertheless seemed to hint of something defective or abnormal in the constitution and blood. But his general aspect and manner were so suggestive of an education and career incongruous with his naval function that when not actively engaged in it he looked like

8 Shawnee chieftain (1768?–1813), leader of a western Indian alliance; he joined the British and was killed in the War of 1812.

9 Titus Oates (1649–1705) was fabricator in 1678 of the alleged "Popish Plot" to seize the English crown for Catholicism by assassinating King Charles and terrorizing London.

a man of high quality, social and moral, who for reasons of his own was keeping incog.[1] Nothing was known of his former life. It might be that he was an Englishman; and yet there lurked a bit of accent in his speech suggesting that possibily he was not such by birth, but through naturalization in early childhood. Among certain grizzled sea gossips of the gundecks and forecastle went a rumor perdue that the master-at-arms was a *chevalier* who had volunteered into the King's navy by way of compounding for some mysterious swindle whereof he had been arraigned at the King's Bench. The fact that nobody could substantiate this report was, of course, nothing against its secret currency. Such a rumor once started on the gundecks in reference to almost anyone below the rank of a commissioned officer would, during the period assigned to this narrative, have seemed not altogether wanting in credibility to the tarry old wiseacres of a man-of-war crew. And indeed a man of Claggart's accomplishments, without prior nautical experience entering the navy at mature life, as he did, and necessarily allotted at the start to the lowest grade in it; a man too who never made allusion to his previous life ashore; these were circumstances which in the dearth of exact knowledge as to his true antecedents opened to the invidious a vague field for unfavorable surmise.

But the sailors' dogwatch gossip concerning him derived a vague plausibility from the fact that now for some period the British navy could so little afford to be squeamish in the matter of keeping up the muster rolls, that not only were press gangs notoriously abroad both afloat and ashore, but there was little or no secret about another matter, namely that the London police were at liberty to capture any able-bodied suspect, any questionable fellow at large and summarily ship him to the dockyard or fleet. Furthermore, even among voluntary enlistments there were instances where the motive thereto partook neither of patriotic impulse nor yet of a random desire to experience a bit of sea life and martial adventure. Insolvent debtors of minor grade, together with the promiscuous lame

---

1 Then a familiar abbreviation for *incognito*, "unrecognized."

ducks of morality found in the navy a convenient and secure refuge. Secure, because once enlisted aboard a King's-ship, they were as much in sanctuary, as the transgressor of the Middle Ages harboring himself under the shadow of the altar. Such sanctioned irregularities, which for obvious reasons the government would hardly think to parade at the time and which consequently, and as affecting the least influential class of mankind, have all but dropped into oblivion, lend color to something for the truth whereof I do not vouch, and hence have some scruple in stating; something I remember having seen in print though the book I cannot recall; but the same thing was personally communicated to me now more than forty years ago by an old pensioner in a cocked hat with whom I had a most interesting talk on the terrace at Greenwich, a Baltimore Negro, a Trafalgar man.[2] It was to this effect: In the case of a warship short of hands whose speedy sailing was imperative, the deficient quota in lack of any other way of making it good, would be eked out by drafts culled direct from the jails. For reasons previously suggested it would not perhaps be easy at the present day directly to prove or dis-prove the allegation. But allowed as a verity, how significant would it be of England's straits at the time confronted by those wars which like a flight of harpies rose shrieking from the din and dust of the fallen Bastille. That era appears measurably clear to us who look back at it, and but read of it. But to the grandfathers of us graybeards, the more thought-ful of them, the genius of it presented an aspect like that of Camoen's[3] Spirit of the Cape, an eclipsing menace mysterious and prodigious. Not America was exempt from apprehension. At the height of Napoleon's unexampled conquests, there were Americans who had fought at Bunker Hill who looked forward to the possibility that the Atlantic might prove no barrier against the ultimate schemes of this French upstart from the revolutionary chaos who seemed in act of fulfilling judgment prefigured in the Apocalypse.

2 *I.e.*, one who had fought at the Battle of Trafalgar (1805), Nelson's fatal victory.

3 Properly, "Camoens," English spelling for "Camoes," Portuguese poet.

But the less credence was to be given to the gundeck talk touching Claggart, seeing that no man holding his office in a man-of-war can ever hope to be popular with the crew. Besides, in derogatory comments upon anyone against whom they have a grudge, or for any reason or no reason mislike, sailors are much like landsmen, they are apt to exaggerate or romance it.

About as much was really known in the *Indomitable's* tars of the master-at-arms' career before entering the service as an astronomer knows about a comet's travels prior to its first observable appearance in the sky. The verdict of the sea quidnuncs[4] has been cited only by way of showing what sort of moral impression the man made upon rude uncultivated natures whose conceptions of human wickedness were necessarily of the narrowest, limited to ideas of vulgar rascality— a thief among the swinging hammocks during a night watch, or the manbrokers and landsharks of the seaports.

It was no gossip, however, but fact, that though, as before hinted, Claggart upon his entrance into the navy was, as a novice, assigned to the least honorable section of a man-of-war's crew, embracing the drudgery, he did not long remain there.

The superior capacity he immediately evinced, his constitutional sobriety, ingratiating deference to superiors, together with a peculiar ferreting genius manifested on a singular occasion, all this capped by a certain austere patriotism abruptly advanced him to the position of master-at-arms.

Of this maritime chief of police the ship's corporals, so called, were the immediate subordinates, and compliant ones; and this, as is to be noted in some business departments ashore, almost to a degree inconsistent with entire moral volition. His place put various converging wires of underground influence under the chief's control, capable when astutely worked through his understrappers of operating to the mysterious discomfort, if nothing worse, of any of the sea commonalty.

---

4 Literally, "what now?" Hence, a busybody, a gossip.

IX

LIFE IN THE FORETOP well agreed with Billy Budd. There, when not actually engaged on the yards yet higher aloft, the topmen, who as such had been picked out for youth and activity, constituted an aerial club lounging at ease against the smaller stun'sails rolled up into cushions, spinning yarns like the lazy gods, and frequently amused with what was going on in the busy world of the decks below. No wonder then that a young fellow of Billy's disposition was well content in such society. Giving no cause of offence to anybody, he was always alert at a call. So in the merchant service it had been with him. But now such a punctiliousness in duty was shown that his topmates would sometimes good-naturedly laugh at him for it. This heightened alacrity had its cause, namely, the impression made upon him by the first formal gangway punishment he had ever witnessed, which befell the day following his impressment. It had been incurred by a little fellow, young, a novice, an afterguardsman absent from his assigned post when the ship was being put about; a dereliction resulting in a rather serious hitch to that maneuver, one demanding instantaneous promptitude in letting go and making fast. When Billy saw the culprit's naked back under the scourge gridironed with red welts, and worse; when he marked the dire expression on the liberated man's face as with his woolen shirt flung over him by the executioner he rushed forward from the spot to bury himself in the crowd, Billy was horrified. He resolved that never through remissness would he make himself liable to such a visitation or do or omit aught that might merit even verbal reproof. What then was his surprise and concern when ultimately he found himself getting into petty trouble occasionally about such matters as the stowage of his bag or something amiss in his hammock, matters under the police oversight of the ship's corporals of the lower decks, and which brought down on him a vague threat from one of them.

So heedful in all things as he was, how could this be? He could not understand it, and it more than vexed him. When he spoke to his young topmates about it they were either lightly incredulous or found something comical in his unconcealed anxiety. "Is it your bag, Billy?" said one, "well, sew yourself up in it, bully boy, and then you'll be sure to know if anybody meddles with it."

Now there was a veteran aboard who because his years began to disqualify him for more active work had been recently assigned duty as mainmastman in his watch, looking to the gear belayed at the rail roundabout that great spar near the deck. At off times the foretopman had picked up some acquaintance with him, and now in his trouble it occurred to him that he might be the sort of person to go to for wise counsel. He was an old Dansker long anglicized in the service, of few words, many wrinkles and some honorable scars. His wizened face, time-tinted and weather-stained to the complexion of an antique parchment, was here and there peppered blue by the chance explosion of a gun cartridge in action. He was an *Agamemnon* man; some two years prior to the time of this story having served under Nelson when but Sir Horatio in that ship immortal in naval memory, and which, dismantled and in part broken up to her bare ribs, is seen a grand skeleton in Haydon's[5] etching. As one of a boarding party from the *Agamemnon* he had received a cut slantwise along one temple and cheek leaving a long pale scar like a streak of dawn's light falling athwart the dark visage. It was on account of that scar and the affair in which it was known that he had received it, as well as from his bluepeppered complexion that the Dansker went among the *Indomitable's* crew by the name of "Board-her-in-the-smoke."

Now the first time that his small weasel eyes happened to light on Billy Budd, a certain grim internal merriment set all his ancient wrinkles into antic play. Was it that his eccentric unsentimental old sapience primitive in its kind saw or thought

5 Benjamin Robert Haydon (1786–1846), English historical painter, much praised by contemporary romantic writers.

it saw something which in contrast with the warship's environment looked oddly incongruous in the handsome sailor? But after slyly studying him at intervals, the old Merlin's equivocal merriment was modified; for now when the twain would meet, it would start in his face a quizzing sort of look, but it would be but momentary and sometimes replaced by an expression of speculative query as to what might eventually befall a nature like that, dropped into a world not without some mantraps and against whose subtleties simple courage, lacking experience and address and without any touch of defensive ugliness, is of little avail; and where such innocence as man is capable of does yet in a moral emergency not always sharpen the faculties or enlighten the will.

However it was the Dansker in his ascetic way rather took to Billy. Nor was this only because of a certain philosophic interest in such a character. There was another cause. While the old man's eccentricities, sometimes bordering on the ursine, repelled the juniors, Billy, undeterred thereby, revering him as a salt hero would make advances, never passing the old Agamemnon-man without a salutation marked by that respect which is seldom lost on the aged however crabbed at times or whatever their station in life.

There was a vein of dry humor, or what not, in the mast-man; and, whether in freak of patriarchal irony touching Billy's youth and athletic frame, or for some other and more recondite reason, from the first in addressing him he always substituted Baby for Billy. The Dansker in fact being the originator of the name by which the foretopman eventually became known aboard ship.

Well then, in his mysterious little difficulty going in quest of the wrinkled one, Billy found him off duty in a dogwatch ruminating by himself seated on a shot box of the upper gun-deck now and then surveying with a somewhat cynical regard certain of the more swaggering promenaders there. Billy recounted his trouble, again wondering how it all happened. The salt seer attentively listened, accompanying the foretop-man's recital with queer twitchings of his wrinkles and problematical little sparkles of his small ferret eyes. Making an end of his story, the foretopman asked, "And now, Dansker, do tell me what you think of it."

The old man, shoving up the front of his tarpaulin and deliberately rubbing the long slant scar at the point where it entered the thin hair, laconically said, "Baby Budd, *Jemmy Legs*"[6] (meaning the master-at-arms) "is down on you."

"*Jemmy Legs!*" ejaculated Billy his welkin eyes expanding; "what for? Why he calls me *the sweet and pleasant young fellow*, they tell me."

"Does he so?" grinned the grizzled one; then said "Ay, Baby Lad, a sweet voice has *Jemmy Legs*."

"No, not always. But to me he has. I seldom pass him but there comes a pleasant word."

"And that's because he's down upon you, Baby Budd."

Such reiteration along with the manner of it, incomprehensible to a novice, disturbed Billy almost as much as the mystery for which he had sought explanation. Something less unpleasingly oracular he tried to extract; but the old sea Chiron[7] thinking perhaps that for the nonce he had sufficiently instructed his young Achilles, pursed his lips, gathered all his wrinkles together and would commit himself to nothing further.

Years, and those experiences which befall certain shrewder men subordinated life-long to the will of superiors, all this had developed in the Dansker the pithy guarded cynicism that was his leading characteristic.

X

THE NEXT DAY an incident served to confirm Billy Budd in his incredulity as to the Dansker's strange summing up of the case submitted. The ship at noon going large before the wind was rolling on her course, and he below at dinner and en-

---

6 "Jimmy-Legs" is still a term of disparagement for the master-at-arms in the United States Navy.

7 In Greek myth, the wisest of the centaurs, skilled in healing, who befriended Achilles and other heroes.

gaged in some sportful talk with the members of his mess, chanced in a sudden lurch to spill the entire contents of his soup pan upon the new scrubbed deck. Claggart, the master-at-arms, official rattan in hand, happened to be passing along the battery in a bay of which the mess was lodged, and the greasy liquid streamed just across his path. Stepping over it, he was proceeding on his way without comment, since the matter was nothing to take notice of under the circumstances, when he happened to observe who it was that had done the spilling. His countenance changed. Pausing, he was about to ejaculate something hasty at the sailor, but checked himself, and pointing down to the streaming soup, playfully tapped him from behind with his rattan, saying in a low musical voice peculiar to him at times "Handsomely done, my lad! And handsome is as handsome did it too!" And with that passed on. Not noted by Billy as not coming within his view was the involuntary smile, or rather grimace, that accompanied Claggart's equivocal words. Aridly it drew down the thin corners of his shapely mouth. But everybody taking his remark as meant for humorous, and at which therefore as coming from a superior they were bound to laugh, "with counterfeited glee"[8] acted accordingly; and Billy tickled, it may be, by the allusion to his being the handsome sailor, merrily joined in; then addressing his messmates exclaimed "There now, who says that Jemmy Legs is down on me!" "And who said he was, Beauty?" demanded one Donald with some surprise. Whereat the foretopman looked a little foolish recalling that it was only one person, Board-her-in-the-smoke, who had suggested what to him was the smoky idea that this master-at-arms was in any peculiar way hostile to him. Meantime that functionary resuming his path must have momentarily worn some expression less guarded than that of the bitter smile, and usurping the face from the heart, some distorting expression perhaps, for a drummer boy heedlessly frolicking along from the opposite direction and chancing to

---

8 *Cf.* Oliver Goldsmith, "The Deserted Village," relating to the severe schoolmaster.

come into light collision with his person was strangely disconcerted by his aspect. Nor was the impression lessened when the official impulsively giving him a sharp cut with the rattan, vehemently exclaimed "Look where you go!"

XI

WHAT WAS THE MATTER with the master-at-arms? And, be the matter what it might, how could it have direct relation to Billy Budd with whom prior to the affair of the spilled soup he had never come into any special contact official or otherwise? What indeed could the trouble have to do with one so little inclined to give offence as the merchant-ship's *peacemaker,* even him who in Claggart's own phrase was "the sweet and pleasant young fellow"? Yes, why should *Jemmy Legs,* to borrow the Dansker's expression, be *down* on the Handsome Sailor? But, at heart and not for nothing, as the late chance encounter may indicate to the discerning, down on him, secretly down on him, he assuredly was.

Now to invent something touching the more private career of Claggart, something involving Billy Budd, of which something the latter should be wholly ignorant, some romantic incident implying that Claggart's knowledge of the young blue-jacket began at some period anterior to catching sight of him on board the seventy-four—all this, not so difficult to do, might avail in a way more or less interesting to account for whatever of enigma may appear to lurk in the case. But in fact there was nothing of the sort. And yet the cause, necessarily to be assumed as the sole one assignable, is in its very realism as much charged with that prime element of Radcliffian[9] romance, *the mysterious,* as any that the ingenuity of the author of the *Mysteries of Udolpho* could devise. For what can more partake of the mysterious than an antipathy spontaneous and profound such as is evoked in certain exceptional mortals by the mere aspect of some other mortal,

---

9 *The Mysteries of Udolpho* (1794), by Ann Radcliffe, was among the most popular of Gothic romances.

however harmless he may be? if not called forth by this very harmlessness itself.

Now there can exist no irritating juxtaposition of dissimilar personalities comparable to that which is possible aboard a great warship fully manned and at sea. There, every day among all ranks almost every man comes into more or less of contact with almost every other man. Wholly there to avoid even the sight of an aggravating object one must needs give it Jonah's toss[1] or jump overboard himself. Imagine how all this might eventually operate on some peculiar human creature the direct reverse of a saint?

But for the adequate comprehending of Claggart by a normal nature these hints are insufficient. To pass from a normal nature to him one must cross "the deadly space between." And this is best done by indirection.

Long ago an honest scholar my senior, said to me in reference to one who like himself is now no more, a man so unimpeachably respectable that against him nothing was ever openly said though among the few something was whispered, "Yes, X—— is a nut not to be cracked by the tap of a lady's fan. You are aware that I am the adherent of no organized religion much less of any philosophy built into a system. Well, for all that, I think that to try and get into X——, enter his labyrinth and get out again, without a clue derived from some source other than what is known as *knowledge of the world*—that were hardly possible, at least for me."

"Why" said I, "X—— however singular a study to some, is yet human, and knowledge of the world assuredly implies the knowledge of human nature, and in most of its varieties."

"Yes, but a superficial knowledge of it, serving ordinary purposes. But for anything deeper, I am not certain whether to know the world and to know human nature be not two distinct branches of knowledge, which while they may coexist in the same heart, yet either may exist with little or nothing of the other. Nay, in an average man of the world, his constant

---

1 In the language of seafaring, the putting overboard of an unlucky person or object.

rubbing with it blunts that fine spiritual insight indispensable to the understanding of the essential in certain exceptional characters, whether evil ones or good. In a matter of some importance I have seen a girl wind an old lawyer about her little finger. Nor was it the dotage of senile love. Nothing of the sort. But he knew law better than he knew the girl's heart. Coke and Blackstone[2] hardly shed so much light into obscure spiritual places as the Hebrew prophets. And who were they? Mostly recluses."

At the time my inexperience was such that I did not quite see the drift of all this. It may be that I see it now. And, indeed, if that lexicon which is based on Holy Writ were any longer popular, one might with less difficulty define and denominate certain phenomenal men. As it is, one must turn to some authority not liable to the charge of being tinctured with the Biblical element.

In a list of definitions included in the authentic translation of Plato, a list attributed to him, occurs this: "Natural Depravity: a depravity according to nature." A definition which though savoring of Calvinism, by no means involves Calvin's dogmas as to total mankind. Evidently its intent makes it applicable but to individuals. Not many are the examples of this depravity which the gallows and jail supply. At any rate for notable instances, since these have no vulgar alloy of the brute in them, but invariably are dominated by intellectuality, one must go elsewhere. Civilization, especially if of the austerer sort, is auspicious to it. It folds itself in the mantle of respectability. It has its certain negative virtues serving as silent auxiliaries. It never allows wine to get within its guard. It is not going too far to say that it is without vices or small sins. There is a phenomenal pride in it that excludes them from anything mercenary or avaricious. In short the depravity here meant partakes nothing of the sordid or sensual. It is serious, but free from acerbity. Though no flatterer of mankind it never speaks ill of it.

---

2 The *Reports* and the *Institutes* of Sir Edward Coke (1552–1634), and the *Commentaries* of Sir William Blackstone (1723–1780) were the foundations of modern British and American jurisprudence.

But the thing which in eminent instances signalizes so exceptional a nature is this: though the man's even temper and discreet bearing would seem to intimate a mind peculiarly subject to the law of reason, not the less in his heart he would seem to riot in complete exemption from that law, having apparently little to do with reason further than to employ it as an ambidexter implement for effecting the irrational. That is to say: Toward the accomplishment of an aim which in wantonness of malignity would seem to partake of the insane, he will direct a cool judgement sagacious and sound.

These men are true madmen, and of the most dangerous sort, for their lunacy is not continuous but occasional, evoked by some special object; it is probably secretive, which is as much to say it is self-contained, so that when, moreover, most active, it is to the average mind not distinguishable from sanity, and for the reason above suggested that whatever its aims may be, and the aim is never declared—the method and the outward proceeding are always perfectly rational.

Now something such an one was Claggart, in whom was the mania of an evil nature, not engendered by vicious training or corrupting books or licentious living, but born with him and innate, in short "a depravity according to nature."

XII

Lawyers, Experts, Clergy
An Episode

BY THE WAY, can it be the phenomenon, disowned or at least concealed, that in some criminal cases puzzles the courts? For this cause have our juries at times not only to endure the prolonged contentions of lawyers with their fees, but also the yet more perplexing strife of the medical experts with theirs? —But why leave it to them? why not subpoena as well the clerical proficients? Their vocation bringing them into peculiar contact with so many human beings, and sometimes in their least guarded hour, in interviews very much more confidential than those of physician and patient; this would seem to qualify them to know something about those intricacies involved in the question of moral responsibility; whether in a given case, say, the crime proceeded from mania in the brain or rabies of the heart. As to any differences among themselves these clerical proficients might develop on the stand, these could hardly be greater than the direct contradictions exchanged between the remunerated medical experts.

Dark sayings are these, some will say. But why? Is it because they somewhat savor of Holy Writ in its phrase "mysteries of iniquity"?[3] If they do, such savor was far from being intended for little will it commend these pages to many a reader of today.

The point of the present story turning on the hidden nature of the master-at-arms has necessitated this chapter. With an added hint or two in connection with the incident at the mess, the resumed narrative must be left to vindicate, as it may, its own credibility.

XIII

Pale ire, envy and despair[4]

THAT CLAGGART'S figure was not amiss, and his face, save the chin, well molded, has already been said. Of these favorable points he seemed not insensible, for he was not only neat but careful in his dress. But the form of Billy Budd was heroic; and if his face was without the intellectual look of the pallid Claggart's, not the less was it lit, like his, from within, though from a different source. The bonfire in his heart made luminous the rose-tan in his cheek.

---

3 *Cf.* II Thessalonians, ii: 7: "For the mystery of iniquity doth already work ..." The words that follow recognize a Satanic and active principle of evil in nature.

4 *Cf.* Milton, *Paradise Lost*, Book IV, 1, 115. Doomed to be man's evil betrayer, the tortured Satan approached Eden, "his face / Thrice changed with pale–ire, envy, and despair."

In view of the marked contrast between the persons of the twain, it is more than probable that when the master-at-arms in the scene last given applied to the sailor the proverb *Handsome is as handsome does;* he there let escape an ironic inkling, not caught by the young sailors who heard it, as to what it was that had first moved him against Billy, namely, his significant personal beauty.

Now envy and antipathy, passions irreconcilable in reason, nevertheless in fact may spring conjoined like Chang and Eng[5] in one birth. Is Envy then such a monster? Well, though many an arraigned mortal has in hopes of mitigated penalty pleaded guilty to horrible actions, did ever anybody seriously confess to envy? Something there is in it universally felt to be more shameful than even felonious crime. And not only does everybody disown it but the better sort are inclined to incredulity when it is in earnest imputed to an intelligent man. But since its lodgment is in the heart not the brain, no degree of intellect supplies a guarantee against it. But Claggart's was no vulgar form of the passion. Nor, as directed toward Billy Budd did it partake of that streak of apprehensive jealousy that marred Saul's visage perturbedly brooding on the comely young David. Claggart's envy struck deeper. If askance he eyed the good looks, cheery health and frank enjoyment of young life in Billy Budd, it was because these went along with a nature that, as Claggart magnetically felt, had in its simplicity never willed malice or experienced the reactionary bite of that serpent. To him, the spirit lodged within Billy, and looking out from his welkins eyes as from windows, that ineffability it was which made the dimple in his dyed cheek, suppled his joints, and dancing in his yellow curls made him pre-eminently the Handsome Sailor. One person excepted the master-at-arms was perhaps the only man in the ship intellectually capable of adequately appreciating the moral phenomenon presented in Billy Budd. And the insight but intensified his passion, which assuming various secret forms

---

5 The original Siamese twins (1811–1874), first exhibited in the United States in 1829.

within him, at times assumed that of cynic disdain—disdain of innocence—to be nothing more than innocent! Yet in an aesthetic way he saw the charm of it, the courageous free-and-easy temper of it, and fain would have shared it, but he despaired of it.

With no power to annul the elemental evil in him, though readily enough he could hide it; apprehending the good, but powerless to be it; a nature like Claggart's surcharged with energy as such natures almost invariably are, what recourse is left to it but to recoil upon itself and like the scorpion for which the Creator alone is responsible, act out to the end the part allotted it?

XIV

PASSION, AND PASSION in its profoundest, is not a thing demanding a palatial stage whereon to play its part. Down among the groundlings, among the beggars and rakers of the garbage, profound passion is enacted. And the circumstances that provoke it, however trivial or mean, are no measure of its power. In the present instance the stage is a scrubbed gun-deck, and one of the external provocations a man-of-war's-man's spilled soup.

Now when the master-at-arms noticed whence came that greasy fluid streaming before his feet, he must have taken it—to some extent wilfully, perhaps—not for the mere accident it assuredly was, but for the sly escape of a spontaneous feeling on Billy's part more or less answering to the antipathy on his own. In effect a foolish demonstration, he must have thought, and very harmless, like the futile kick of a heifer, which yet were the heifer a shod stallion, would not be so harmless. Even so was it that into the gall of Claggart's envy he infused the vitriol of his contempt. But the incident confirmed to him certain telltale reports purveyed to his ear by *Squeak*, one of his more cunning corporals, a grizzled little man, so nicknamed by the sailors on account of his squeaky voice, and sharp visage ferreting about the dark corners of the lower decks after interlopers, satirically suggesting to them the idea of a rat in a cellar.

From his chief's employing him as an implicit tool in laying little traps for the worriment of the foretopman—for it was from the master-at-arms that the petty persecutions heretofore adverted to had proceeded—the corporal having naturally enough concluded that his master could have no love for the sailor, made it his business, faithful understrapper that he was, to foment the ill blood by perverting to his chief certain innocent frolics of the good-natured foretopman, besides inventing for his mouth sundry contumelious epithets he claimed to have overheard him let fall. The master-at-arms never suspected the veracity of these reports, more especially as to the epithets, for he well knew how secretly unpopular may become a master-at-arms, at least a master-at-arms of those days zealous in his function, and how the blue-jackets shoot at him in private their raillery and wit; the nickname by which he goes among them (*Jemmy Legs*) implying under the form of merriment their cherished disrespect and dislike.

But in view of the greediness of hate for patrolmen it hardly needed a purveyor to feed Claggart's passion. An uncommon prudence is habitual with the subtler depravity, for it has everything to hide. And in case of an injury but suspected, its secretiveness voluntarily cuts it off from enlightenment or disillusion; and, not unreluctantly, action is taken upon surmise as upon certainty. And the retaliation is apt to be in monstrous disproportion to the supposed offence; for when in anybody was revenge in its exactions aught else but an inordinate usurer. But how with Claggart's conscience? For though consciences are unlike as foreheads, every intelligence, not excluding the scriptural devils who "believe and tremble," has one. But Claggart's conscience being but the lawyer to his will, made ogres of trifles, probably arguing that the motive imputed to Billy in spilling the soup just when he did, together with the epithets alleged, these, if nothing more, made a strong case against him; nay, justified animosity into a sort of retributive righteousness. The Pharisee is the Guy Fawkes[6] prowling in the hid chambers underlying the Claggarts. And they can really form no conception of an unreciprocated malice. Probably, the master-at-arms' clandestine persecution of Billy was started to try the temper of the man; but it had not developed any quality in him that enmity could make official use of or even pervert into plausible self-justification; so that the occurrence at the mess, petty if it were, was a welcome one to that peculiar conscience assigned to be the private mentor of Claggart; and, for the rest, not improbably it put him upon new experiments.

XV

NOT MANY DAYS after the last incident narrated something befell Billy Budd that more graveled him than aught that had previously occurred.

It was a warm night for the latitude; and the foretopman, whose watch at the time was properly below, was dozing on the uppermost deck whither he had ascended from his hot hammock one of hundreds suspended so closely wedged together over a lower gundeck that there was little or no swing to them. He lay as in the shadow of a hillside, stretched under the lee of the booms, a piled ridge of spare spars amidships between foremast and mainmast and among which the ship's largest boat, the launch, was stowed. Alongside of three other slumberers from below, he lay near that end of the booms which approaches the foremast; his station aloft on duty as a foretopman being just over the deck station of the forecastlemen, entitling him according to usage to make himself more or less at home in that neighborhood.

Presently he was stirred into semiconsciousness by somebody, who must have previously sounded the sleep of the others, touching his shoulder, and then as the foretopman

---

6 Principal conspirator in the Gunpowder Plot (1604–1605) to blow up the British Houses of Parliament.

raised his head, breathing into his ear in a quick whisper, "Slip into the lee forechains, Billy; there is something in the wind. Don't speak. Quick, I will meet you there," and disappeared

Now Billy like sundry other essentially good-natured ones had some of the weaknesses inseparable from essential good nature; and among these was a reluctance, almost an incapacity of plumply saying *no* to an abrupt proposition not obviously absurd, on the face of it, nor obviously unfriendly, nor iniquitous. And being of warm blood he had not the phlegm tacitly to negative any proposition by unresponsive inaction. Like his sense of fear, his apprehension as to aught outside of the honest and natural was seldom very quick. Besides, upon the present occasion, the drowse from his sleep still hung upon him.

However it was, he mechanically rose, and sleepily wondering what could be in the wind, betook himself to the designated place, a narrow platform, one of six, outside of the high bulwarks and screened by the great dead-eyes and multiple columned lanyards of the shrouds and backstays; and, in a great warship of that time, of dimensions commensurate with the hull's magnitude; a tarry balcony in short overhanging the sea, and so secluded that one mariner of the *Indomitable,* a nonconformist old tar of a serious turn, made it even in daytime his private oratory.

In this retired nook the stranger soon joined Billy Budd. There was no moon as yet; a haze obscured the starlight. He could not distinctly see the stranger's face. Yet from something in the outline and carriage, Billy took him to be, and correctly, for one of the afterguard.

"Hist! Billy," said the man in the same quick cautionary whisper as before; "You were impressed, weren't you? Well, so was I"; and he paused, as to mark the effect. But Billy not knowing exactly what to make of this said nothing. Then the other; "We are not the only impressed ones, Billy. There's a gang of us— Couldn't you—help—at a pinch?"

"What do you mean?" demanded Billy here thoroughly shaking off his drowse.

"Hist, hist!" the hurried whisper now growing husky, "see here," and the man held up two small objects faintly twinkling in the nightlight, "see, they are yours, Billy, if you'll only——"

But Billy broke in, and in his resentful eagerness to deliver himself his vocal infirmity somewhat intruded: "D-D-Damme, I don't know what you are d-d-driving at, or what you mean, but you had better g-g-go where you belong!" For the moment the fellow, as confounded, did not stir; and Billy springing to his feet, said, "If you d-don't start I'll t-t-toss you back over the r-rail!" There was no mistaking this and the mysterious emissary decamped, disappearing in the direction of the shadow of the booms.

"Hallo, what's the matter?" here came growling from a forecastleman awakened from his deck doze by Billy's raised voice. And as the foretopman reappeared and was recognized by him; "Ah, Beauty, is it you? Well, something must have been the matter for you st-st-stuttered."

"Oh," rejoined Billy, now mastering the impediment; "I found an afterguardsman in our part of the ship here and I bid him be off where he belongs."

"And is that all you did about it, foretopman?" gruffly demanded another, an irascible old fellow of brick-colored visage and hair, and who was known to his associate forecastlemen as *Red Pepper;* "Such sneaks I should like to marry to the gunner's daughter!" by that expression meaning that he would like to subject them to disciplinary castigation over a gun.

However, Billy's rendering of the matter satisfactorily accounted to these inquiries for the brief commotion, since of all the sections of a ship's company the forecastlemen, veterans for the most part and bigoted in their sea prejudices, are the most jealous in resenting territorial encroachments, especially on the part of any of the afterguard, of whom they have but a sorry opinion, chiefly landsmen, never going aloft except to reef or furl the mainsail, and in no wise competent to handle a marlinspike or turn in a *dead-eye,* say.

XVI

THIS INCIDENT SORELY puzzled Billy Budd. It was an entirely new experience; the first time in his life that he had ever been personally approached in underhand intriguing fashion. Prior to this encounter he had known nothing of the afterguardsman, the two men being stationed wide apart, one forward and aloft during his watch, the other on deck and aft.

What could it mean? And could they really be guineas, those two glittering objects the interloper had held up to his eyes? Where could the fellow get guineas? Why even buttons are not so plentiful at sea. The more he turned the matter over, the more he was nonplussed, and made uneasy and discomforted. In his disgustful recoil from an overture which though he but ill comprehended he instinctively knew must involve evil of some sort, Billy Budd was like a young horse fresh from the pasture suddenly inhaling a vile whiff from some chemical factory and by repeated snortings tries to get it out of his nostrils and lungs. This frame of mind barred all desire of holding further parley with the fellow, even were it but for the purpose of gaining some enlightenment as to his design in approaching him. And yet he was not without natural curiosity to see how such a visitor in the dark would look in broad day.

He espied him the following afternoon in his first dogwatch below, one of the smokers on that forward part of the upper gundeck allotted to the pipe.[7] He recognized him by his general cut and build, more than by his round freckled face and glassy eyes of pale blue, veiled with lashes all but white. And yet Billy was a bit uncertain whether indeed it were he—yonder chap about his own age chatting and laughing in freehearted way, leaning against a gun; a genial young fellow enough to look at, and something of a rattlebrain, to all appearance. Rather chubby too for a sailor, even an after-

---

7 A portion of the forward gundeck where the sailors were allowed to smoke.

guardsman. In short the last man in the world, one would think, to be overburdened with thoughts, especially those perilous thoughts that must needs belong to a conspirator in any serious project, or even to the underling of such a conspirator.

Although Billy was not aware of it, the fellow, with a sidelong watchful glance had perceived Billy first, and then noting that Billy was looking at him, thereupon nodded a familiar sort of friendly recognition as to an old acquaintance, without interrupting the talk he was engaged in with the group of smokers. A day or two afterwards chancing in the evening promenade on a gundeck, to pass Billy, he offered a flying word of good-fellowship as it were, which by its unexpectedness, and equivocalness under the circumstances so embarrassed Billy that he knew not how to respond to it, and let it go unnoticed.

Billy was now left more at a loss than before. The ineffectual speculation into which he was led was so disturbingly alien to him that he did his best to smother it. It never entered his mind that here was a matter which from its extreme questionableness, it was his duty as a loyal blue-jacket to report in the proper quarter. And, probably, had such a step been suggested to him, he would have been deterred from taking it by the thought, one of novice magnanimity, that it would savor overmuch of the dirty work of a telltale. He kept the thing to himself. Yet upon one occasion, he could not forbear a little disburdening himself to the old Dansker, tempted thereto perhaps by the influence of a balmy night when the ship lay becalmed; the twain, silent for the most part, sitting together on deck, their heads propped against the bulwarks. But it was only a partial and anonymous account that Billy gave, the unfounded scruples above referred to preventing full disclosure to anybody. Upon hearing Billy's version, the sage Dansker seemed to divine more than he was told; and after a little meditation during which his wrinkles were pursed as into a point, quite effacing for the time that quizzing expression his face sometimes wore—"Didn't I say so, Baby Budd?"

Reader's Supplement

to

BILLY BUDD

HERMAN MELVILLE (1819–1891)

BIOGRAPHICAL BACKGROUND

The present volume contains the last short story or novelette, *Billy Budd,* which Melville wrote during the years 1888–1891, but which was published only in 1924. Melville's first novel, *Typee,* appeared in 1846. Between these two books there is, of course, the famous *Moby Dick;* and between them also is Melville's enigmatic, tormented and tragic career as one of the few great American fiction writers, immensely popular at the outset and gradually condemned to the neglect and oblivion that extended for a quarter of a century after his death.

During this period his books were not reprinted; his name was stricken from that illustrious roster of the New England transcendentalists, which included Thoreau, Emerson and Hawthorne. Melville, who belonged to them in one sense surely, was as mute as Walt Whitman, who had started with Emerson's glowing approval. That is to say, our primary novelist and our prime poet of the period— the writers who formed the real bridge between the two great American literary revivals—were virtually taboo. Why? In Melville's case, at least, it is the purpose here to suggest a few possible reasons.

Coming from a respectable New York family of Dutch and English stock, but one that the father's bankruptcy and death had brought into poverty and disrepute, Melville went to sea at nineteen. He never forgot this wealth of physical and material experience, which was denied to the more scholarly or reclusive New Englanders. This was in 1838. Three years later he shipped aboard the *Acushnet* for a South Sea whaling cruise that was to last four years. It was during this cruise that, with the "Toby" of *Typee,* he deserted the whaler at Nukuheva in the Marquesas

Islands and established his somewhat enforced residence among the "savage" and cannibalistic Typees (or Taipis, in modern usage). From this experience came the first modern novel of the South Seas, immensely popular in its own day and still remarkably fresh, entertaining and acute.

Right here, indeed, occurred Melville's deep and almost traumatic split from the central values of that western European and American "civilization," which just then in the mid-nineteenth century saw itself destined for endless aeons of "progress." How sharply, clearly, definitively *Typee* strikes this note, which becomes the central Melvillian theme of primitive nature *versus society*. For Taipian culture was the original Eden—or the pre-Edenite community of love and friendship and joy—which civilization had remembered, yearned for and could never achieve. For these "frightful savages" had turned out to be the most gentle, considerate, affectionate, happy, natural and satisfying people. Their "social order" was splendidly regulated to afford the minimum of social pressure. There was no law to constrain their behavior; no police force, no crime. Were they, in short, the most accomplished and urbane race of people in the South Seas—in the whole world perhaps? Still the novel's hero had to leave them. He was branded by the mark of Adam, the knowledge of evil, sin and corruption. He himself was the product and the victim of centuries of civilization. He could not remain, nor could he ever (except in his memory, in his values, in his later judgments) return to Typee.

And meanwhile what happened to Melville himself? *Typee* was part of a whole cluster of early works. *Omoo* (1847), *Redburn* (1849) and *White Jacket* (1850) all contributed to his early popular fame. *Moby Dick* (1851) was, as we know now, the masterpiece, but in its own time it was attacked and criticized for its uncouth form, its verbosity, its irrelevancies, its extravagant emotions centered around the cruise of an ordinary whaling ship—and perhaps for other things not entirely mentionable to the increasingly staid and proper literary conscience of New England and New York. By this time Melville had married the daughter of an eminent Boston judge; he had settled down to that respectable domestic life that at heart he abhorred. For a time he lived near Pittsfield, Massachusetts, next to his intimate friend and literary idol, Hawthorne, who had both secret and expressed reservations as to Melville and Melville's work. And *Pierre,* in 1852, suddenly completed Melville's downfall.

This was a curious and often distressing romance-fantasy of incest and moral disintegration, in which Melville was nevertheless trying to penetrate his own (or man's) deepest buried nature and hidden, primitive affections—and it received even more critical abuse for its lack of form and for its revelation of things better left unsaid and unknown. During the writing of *Moby Dick,* Melville was filled with premonitions of his own decline and disintegration. Was *Pierre* simply the record of this, or even a deliberate attempt, as it were, at literary suicide? He published, at any rate, one more volume of fine short stories, *The Piazza Tales,* in 1856. The two remaining novels were inferior; his sales were poor; his books were not reprinted; he took to writing indifferent poetry, which he published at his own, or his uncle's, expense. For over thirty years he worked as a customs inspector in New York, as a forgotten and unknown, if not dishonored, man. Until, that is, the three last years of his life when he wrote *Billy Budd,* one of the great stories of the world.

HISTORICAL BACKGROUND

The year 1797, the year of this narrative, belongs to a period which, as every thinker now feels, involved a crisis for Christendom not exceeded in its undetermined momentousness at the time by any other era whereof there is record. The opening proposition made by the Spirit of that Age involved rectification of the Old World's hereditary wrongs. In France, to some extent, this was bloodily effected. But what then? Straightway the Revolution itself became a wrongdoer, one more oppressive than the kings. Under Napoleon it enthroned upstart kings, and initiated that prolonged agony of continual war whose final throe was Waterloo. During those years not the wisest could have foreseen that the outcome of all would be what to some thinkers apparently it has since turned out to be—a political advance along nearly the whole line for Europeans.

Now, as elsewhere hinted, it was something caught from the Revolutionary Spirit that at Spithead emboldened the man-of-war's men to rise against real abuses, long-standing ones, and afterwards at the Nore to make inordinate and aggressive demands—successful resistance to which was confirmed only when the ringleaders were hung for an admonitory spectacle to the anchored fleet. Yet in a way analogous to the operation of the Revolution at large—the Great Mutiny, though by Englishmen naturally deemed

---

The manuscript title is "Billy Budd / Sailor / (an inside narrative)"; and beneath it appears the following: "Dedicated to Jack Chase, Englishman, wherever that great heart may now be here on earth or harbored in paradise. Captain of the maintop in the year 1843 in the U.S. frigate *United States*."

Adapted from a Preface that appeared in the first publication of this work, under the title *Billy Budd, Foretopman*, in 1924.

monstrous at the time, doubtless gave the first latent prompting to most important reforms in the British navy.

Note: The page references on the following pages direct your attention to passages in the text (T for Top of page, M for Middle, and B for Bottom).

PICTORIAL BACKGROUND

*In the time before steamships . . . a stroller along the docks
of any considerable seaport would occasionally have his attention arrested by a group of bronzed mariners, man-of-war's
men or merchant-sailors in holiday attire ashore on liberty.
. . . In Liverpool, now half a century ago I saw under the
shadow of the great dingy street-wall of Prince's Dock. . . .
(p. 5T)*

LIVERPOOL HARBOR AND DOCKS—1790's

Billy Budd . . . aged twenty-one, a foretopman of the British fleet toward the close of the last decade of the eighteenth century. . . . It was not very long . . . that he had entered the King's service, having been impressed on the Narrow Seas from a homeward-bound English merchantman into a seventy-four outward-bound, H.M.S. Indomitable . . . short of her proper complement of men. (p. 7T)

IMPRESSMENT OF SEAMEN—LATE 1700's

Aboard the Indomitable *our merchant-sailor was forthwith rated as an able seaman and assigned to the starboard watch of the foretop. He was soon at home in the service, not at all disliked for his unpretentious good looks and a sort of genial happy-go-lucky air. No merrier man in his mess: in marked contrast to certain other individuals. . . . (p. 12T)*

BRITISH "TAR" OF THE 1700's

It was the summer of 1797. In the April of that year had occurred the commotion at Spithead followed in May by a second and yet more serious outbreak in the fleet at the Nore. The latter is known, and without exaggeration in the epithet, as the Great Mutiny. It was indeed a demonstration more menacing to England than the contemporary manifestoes. . . . (p. 16B)

TERMS BEING PRESENTED TO ADMIRAL BUCKNER IN THE MUTINY AT NORE—1797

Captain the Honorable Edward Fairfax Vere, to give his full title, was a bachelor of forty or thereabouts, a sailor of distinction even in a time prolific of renowned seamen. Though allied to the higher nobility his advancement had not been altogether owing to influences connected with that circumstance. He had seen much service. . . . (p. 23T)

A CAPTAIN IN THE BRITISH NAVY—ABOUT 1800

This was John Claggart, the master-at-arms. But that sea title may to landsmen seem somewhat equivocal. Originally doubtless that petty officer's function was the instruction of the men in the use of arms, sword or cutlas. But very long ago . . . that function ceased; the master-at-arms of a great warship becoming a sort of chief of police. . . . (p. 27T)

BRITISH PETTY OFFICER—LATE 1700's

Life in the foretop well agreed with Billy Budd. There, when not actually engaged on the yards yet higher aloft, the topmen, who as such had been picked out for youth and activity, constituted an aerial club lounging at ease . . . spinning yarns like the lazy gods, and frequently amused with what was going on in the busy world of the decks below. (p. 31T)

"TOPMEN" ALOFT—BRITISH VESSEL, 1700's

When Billy saw the culprit's naked back under the scourge gridironed with red welts, and worse; when he marked the dire expression on the liberated man's face as with his woolen shirt flung over him by the executioner he rushed forward from the spot to bury himself in the crowd, Billy was horrified. He resolved that never. . . . (p. 31M)

A FLOGGING ABOARD SHIP—EARLY 1800's

The ship at noon going large before the wind was rolling on her course, and he below at dinner and engaged in some sportful talk with the members of his mess, chanced in a sudden lurch to spill the entire contents of his soup pan upon the new scrubbed deck. Claggart . . . happened to be passing along the battery in a bay of which the mess was lodged. . . . (p. 34B)

SEAMEN'S MESS—LATE 1700's

And yet he was not without natural curiosity to see how such a visitor in the dark would look in broad day.

He espied him the following afternoon in his first dogwatch below, one of the smokers on that forward part of the upper gundeck allotted to the pipe. He recognized him by his general cut and build. . . . (p. 47M)

GUNDECK—BRITISH WARSHIP, EARLY 1800's

This order Billy in silence obeyed. Then going to the cabin door where it opened on the quarterdeck, Captain Vere said to the sentry without, "Tell somebody to send Albert here." When the lad appeared his master so contrived it that he should not catch sight of the prone one. "Albert," he said to him, "tell the surgeon I wish to see him. . . ." (p. 63M)

SHIP'S SURGEON—1700's

All being quickly in readiness, Billy Budd was arraigned, Captain Vere necessarily appearing as the sole witness in the case, and as such temporarily sinking his rank, though singularly maintaining it in a matter apparently trivial, namely, that he testified from the ship's weather side, with that object having caused the court to sit on the lee side. (p. 68M)

A COURT MARTIAL AT SEA—1800's

To be prepared for burial Claggart's body was delivered to certain petty-officers of his mess. And here, not to clog the sequel with lateral matters, it may be added that at a suitable hour, the master-at-arms was committed to the sea with every funeral honor properly belonging to his naval grade. (p. 79B)

BURIAL AT SEA—1800's

*The chaplain coming to see him . . . and perceiving no sign
that he was conscious of his presence . . . withdrew for the
time. . . . But in the small hours he came again. And the
prisoner . . . noticed his approach and civilly, all but cheerfully, welcomed him. But it was to little purpose that . . . the
good man sought to bring Billy Budd to some godly understanding that he must die. . . . (p. 82M)*

SHIP'S CHAPLAIN CONDUCTING SERVICES—1800's

At sea in the old time, the execution by halter of a military sailor was generally from the foreyard. In the present instance, for special reasons the mainyard was assigned. Under an arm of that lee yard the prisoner was presently brought up, the chaplain attending him. . . . Brief speech indeed he had with the condemned one. . . . (p. 85B)

PREPARATIONS FOR HANGING AT SEA—1797

For suddenly the drumbeat to quarters, which familiar sound happening at least twice every day, had upon the present occasion a signal peremptoriness in it. True martial discipline long continued superinduces in average man a sort of impulse of docility whose operation at the official sound of command much resembles in its promptitude the effect of an instinct. (p. 90M)

A DRUMBEAT ABOARD SHIP—1800's

*On the return passage to the English fleet from the detached
cruise during which occurred the events already recorded, the
Indomitable fell in with the Athéiste. An engagement ensued;
during which Captain Vere in the act of putting his ship
alongside the enemy . . . was hit by a musketball. . . . (p. 91B)*

BRITISH WARSHIP ENGAGED—1790's

Not long before death while lying under the influence of that magical drug which soothing the physical frame mysteriously operates on the subtler element in man, he was heard to murmur words inexplicable to his attendant—"Billy Budd, Billy Budd." That these were not the accents of remorse, would seem clear. . . . (p. 92M)

FATALLY WOUNDED NAVAL OFFICER—1794

VISUAL GLOSSARY

1—cutlas (p. 27T)   3—hawsers (p. 95M)
2—halter (p. 85B)   4—scourge (p. 31M)

5–halyard (p. 13M)   7–poopdeck (p. 68T)
6–yardarm (p. 6B)   8–quarterdeck (p. 7M)

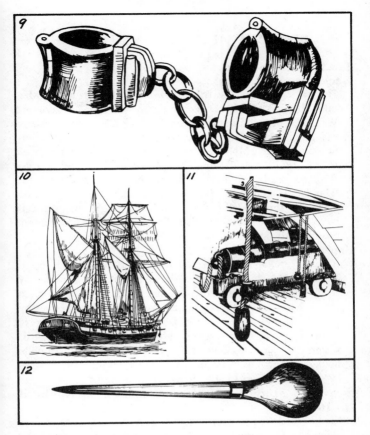

9—darbies (p. 94B)   11—carronade (p. 68M)
10—frigate (p. 54M)   12—marlinspike (p. 46B)

LITERARY ALLUSIONS AND NOTES

Jack Chase (footnote to Historical Background, p. 5B):

He was captain of the frigate *United States,* on which Melville shipped in 1842. According to biographer Raymond Weaver, "Melville's admiration for Jack Chase was perhaps the happiest wholehearted surrender he ever gave to any human being." Melville first spoke of Chase in his book *White Jacket.* According to Weaver, "The novel, *Billy Budd,* is built around the character of Jack Chase, the 'Handsome Sailor.'" Other critics have commented on Chase as the model for Billy Budd, though other models have been cited, notably Elisha Small, the sailor who figured prominently in the *Somers* incident.

Hercules (p. 13M):

Called Herakles in Greek, he was one of the twin sons of Zeus, and from his cradle showed unusual prowess by strangling two huge serpents sent to destroy him. As a Greek hero, he is represented as overcoming his enemies by both craft and superior strength. A king gave him twelve labors to perform, of seemingly impossible difficulty, all of which he accomplished with daring and skill. Melville helped to show Billy Budd's superiority among his fellows by comparing him to the "heroic strong man."

the Great Mutiny and the commotion at Spithead (p. 16B):

In 1797, Britain's situation was serious. Her continental allies had either been defeated or had withdrawn from the war; the French were masters of western Europe. The fleets of France, Spain, and Holland were ranged against Great Britain. Though the Spanish line was broken at the battle of Cape St. Vincent in February of 1797, the whole naval position in the North Sea was threatened by mutinies in the fleet. The first mutiny occurred at Spithead, on April 15th, fired by the grievances of the seamen who were badly fed, seldom paid, brutally punished to maintain discipline, and often forced into the navy by the press-gang. The authorities granted the sailors' claims, and a bill was passed through Parliament to raise seamen's pay. News of the vote, and a royal pardon, quelled the mutiny. The results encouraged an outbreak on May 12th in the North Sea fleet blockading the Dutch coast. Mutineers seized the ships and sailed back to the Thames estuary, with their headquarters at the Nore. After a month, the men returned to their duties. The ringleader and eighteen others were hanged. The two events play an important part throughout *Billy Budd*. Melville makes them the subject of what can be constituted a separate essay in the story (see pp. 16–18 ff). They influence the thinking of Captain Vere during the drum-head court trial and prompt him to speak out for strict adherence to military discipline to avert a repetition of the Nore mutiny on board the *Indomitable*.

Montaigne (p. 25M):

Michel de Montaigne was a sixteenth-century French essayist. He is regarded as the first Frenchman to adopt the system of free criticism in regard to philosophic questions. He loved peace, public order, and submission to absolute power; he gave sovereign place in his philosophy to reason. He had an overriding respect, according to one critic, for law, however fallible, as against personal judgment, and this is interesting when we note how Melville singled out Montaigne as a favorite author with Captain Vere. What Vere responded to in Montaigne, Melville makes clear, is not opinions, but an attitude—honest, realistic, "Free from cant and convention." Montaigne argued the wisdom of ordering human conduct by fixed principles and insisted that men must live by definite laws superior to the will; these laws are civil statutes as distinct from so-called laws of conscience.

Merlin (p. 33T):

He was the celebrated magician of the Arthurian legends who reared King Arthur to the time he became king. He was both loved and feared for his wisdom and magical powers. Melville's reference to the Dansker as an "old

Merlin" was merely another indication that he was regarded
as both a wise and a mysterious man himself.

Achilles (p. 34M):

This noble and valiant Greek warrior was not supposed to
be subject to pain or death, except for the heel of his foot,
where he could be wounded. Achilles fought heroically in
the Trojan War and did meet death from a poisoned arrow
in the heel of his foot. Since Melville has just referred to
the Dansker as Chiron, the centaur who befriended Achilles,
then Billy Budd may be taken as the young and supposedly
invulnerable Achilles who can yet be fatally undone.

Calvinism (p. 38M):

This is a reference to the religious sect named after its
French founder, John Calvin. Its precepts are mainly found
in Calvin's work *The Institutes of the Christian Religion*.
Calvinism taught the doctrine of predestination, that is, that
man, from birth, was predestined by God for salvation or
damnation. The "elect," or "saints," would go to heaven,
and the others to hell, without regard to their deeds or their
manner of life. However, the leading of a good life was
evidence that one belonged to the "elect." Melville states
that Plato's definition of "Natural Depravity," which Melville believes is inherent in Claggart, is a term which savors
of Calvinism, but would be more applicable to individuals
in Plato, than to total mankind in Calvin's teachings.

Saul and David (p. 41M):

Saul and David appear in the First Book of Samuel in the
Bible. Saul was anointed the first king of Israel. David was
a shepherd boy who became Saul's armorbearer; he used
to refresh Saul by his harp-playing. David fought Goliath,
the giant of the Philistines, and vanquished him with his
slingshot. David and Jonathan, Saul's son, made a covenant
of devoted friendship. Saul, meanwhile, became envious of
David's increasing favor with the Israelites and even sought
to slay David with his spear on two occasions. Even so,
David became a captain in Saul's army and wed Saul's
daughter Michal. However, David finally chose to flee from
Saul's displeasure and wandered over the land. Saul at last
killed himself with his sword after a defeat by the Phi-

listines, in which Jonathan was also slain; his head was cut off and exhibited to the Philistine people. David was then anointed king of Judah. Melville, by saying that Claggart's envy of Billy struck even deeper than the "apprehensive jealousy" of Saul for David, is making a most powerful analogy.

Pharisee (pp. 43B–44T):

The name "Pharisee" in the Bible means "Separated" or "Separatist," but it has come to be almost synonymous with that of "hypocrite," mainly because of Christ's address to the Pharisees (Matthew XXIII. 27): "Woe unto you, scribes and Pharisees, hypocrites! because you are like whited sepulchres, which outwardly appear to men beautiful, but are within full of dead men's bones and of all uncleanness." Christ also related the parable of the Pharisee and the Publican (Luke XVIII. 9–14), in which the humble Publican was praised in opposition to the proud Pharisee who thanked God that he was better than other men. Melville is referring to Claggart's justifying his animosity towards Billy as a sort of retributive righteousness. He is saying that the Pharisee, the hypocrite, like vice parading as virtue, is the Guy Fawkes, the explosive agent, prowling deep below Claggart's awareness.

Delphic (p. 49M):

This refers to the Greek shrine of Apollo, called the oracle at Delphi because it was located at Delphi on the island of Delos. It was one of several places regarded as the center of the earth and was held to be traditionally holy. Pilgrims came to the shrine from all over the world. They asked questions, delivered to a priestess seated at the shrine, who went into a trance before she spoke. What she answered was regarded as the Truth, though the answers often seemed enigmatic or were couched in obscure terms and had to be deciphered and interpreted by the listener. Melville compares the Dansker's oracles to the Delphic oracles in that they share a certain obscurity.

man of sorrows (p. 51M):

The phrase can be found in the Bible, the Book of Isaias the Prophet (LIII. 3). In Isaias it is part of a prophecy of

the passion of Christ: ". . . despised, and the most abject
of men, a man of sorrows, and acquainted with infirmity . . ." Isaias goes on to speak of Christ as one who has
borne the sorrows of men, who was bruised for the sins of
men, and who was led as a sheep to the slaughter. Melville
says that sometimes Claggart would regard Billy with a
meditative and melancholic expression, at which times
Claggart would look like the man of sorrows. This description of Melville's has been used by the critics to render
Claggart's portrayal a more sympathetic one. One critic has
said that Claggart seems at moments to *be* the "man of sorrows" (italicized word not the critic's), but this seems to
extend the analogy too far.

Jacob and Joseph (p. 59M):

Jacob and Joseph are found in the Bible, the Book of
Genesis. Jacob was one of the patriarchs, son of Isaac and
descendent of Abraham. Later God changed Jacob's name
to that of Israel, and gave to him and his seed the Promised
Land. Jacob's son Joseph was his favorite because he had
been born in Jacob's old age. Joseph's brothers envied him,
and when he told them of dreams wherein he was worshiped
by sheaves and by the sun, moon, and stars, they plotted
to kill him. One brother, Reuben, saved him from blood-
shed. Instead the brothers cast Joseph into an empty cistern
and then sold him into slavery in Egypt. They sent his
tunic, which they had stripped from him, dipped in goat's
blood, to Jacob, who then believed his son dead. Joseph
later found favor with the Pharaoh of Egypt and was
reunited with Jacob and with his brothers, whom he for-
gave. Melville refers to Claggart, watching Captain Vere for
a reaction to his accusation of Billy Budd, much as the
spokesman of Joseph's brothers might have looked for
Jacob's reaction to the sight of his son's bloodstained coat.
In both instances, deception and trickery were involved,
and both were triggered by envy.

vestal priestess (p. 62T):

The Vestal Virgins were Roman virgins who were to keep
the holy fire of early Rome burning in the temple of Vesta.
During their term of office, they were not allowed to marry.

If they desecrated their sacred office in any way, they were punished by being buried alive. Hence Melville's forceful reference to Billy's facial expression, like that of one struggling against suffocation, when he is attempting to answer Claggart's accusation.

Ananias (p. 63B):

The character of Ananias appears in the Acts of the Apostles in the Bible (V. 1–10) written by St. Luke about 63 A.D. The Acts narrate the chief events in the history of the infant Church and trace the spread of the Church. In The Acts, Ananias and his wife Sapphira sold a piece of land and brought only a part of its price to the apostles. Peter confronted Ananias with his fraud and told him that he had not lied to men, but to God. Hearing this, Ananias died; three hours later, his wife died also after being confronted with her connivance in fraud and with the news of her husband's death. Captain Vere, well conversant with the Scriptures, likens Claggart's death to that of Ananias, whose fraud before God was met with instantaneous death and "divine judgment." By so likening the two deaths, Vere would seem to say that justice had been done to Claggart.

drum-head court (p. 64M):

According to the standard definition, it is a court-martial held round an upturned drum for summary trial of offenses during military operations. In *Billy Budd,* it is similar, though not held round a drum, in its immediate hearing and judgment of Billy's offense.

"mystery of iniquity" (p. 70B):

This phrase occurs in the Bible, the Second Epistle of St. Paul the Apostle to the Thessalonians (II. 7): "For the mystery of iniquity is already at work; providing only that he who is at present restraining it, does still restrain, until he is gotten out of the way." Paul is beseeching the Thessalonians not to fear the Second Coming of Christ, which could not take place until the Antichrist appeared. According to the biblical footnote to the phrase, as it appears in the Confraternity Edition of the New Testament, 1957, the "mystery of iniquity" is the evil power of which the Antichrist is to be the public exponent and champion. "He who is at present restraining it" is suggested by some to be Michael the Archangel. Captain Vere refers to the "mystery of iniquity" in answer to a soldier's seeking to clarify the mysterious elements in Billy Budd's case before the court. Again Vere reveals his scriptural awareness, and his remark could be construed, if he is basing it on knowledge of the context and nature of the complete biblical quote, to mean that Claggart is the figure of the Antichrist and Billy is the obstacle who sought to restrain him. Again "iniquity" could hearken back to Melville's description of Claggart as having been born with "a depravity according to nature" (p. 39M). And, again, the terms "mystery" or "mysterious" are typical with Melville, who liked to deal with enigmas and ambiguities.

Mutiny Act (p. 74M):

Passed in 1689, it began by reaffirming the illegality of courts-martial and military discipline, and conferred upon King William the authority to provide for the exercise of such extraordinary jurisdiction for six months. It was triggered by the mutiny of an English regiment at Ipswich in the first year of William's reign. The act was regularly renewed, but never for longer than a year. It figures prominently in Billy's trial, as Captain Vere counsels the court that they are to proceed under its provisions. It is this law, Vere says, which forces Englishmen to fight for the king against their will.

Somers incident (p. 76T):

A reference to the execution at sea, in 1842, on board the brig *Somers,* of midshipman Philip Spencer and two seamen, by Commander Alexander Slidell Mackenzie. Spencer was eighteen years old, the son of President Tyler's Secretary of War. He was reportedly plotting a mutiny on board the *Somers,* a training ship at the time engaged on a schooling cruise. Witnesses to Spencer's talk of mutiny had not taken him seriously, as he was known to be given to boasting and had a vivid imagination. Inquiry was later made in the case because of the challenge of Spencer's father as to the justice of the affair. Mackenzie was acquitted, but the affair had imprinted itself in the public mind. One of

Melville's cousins, Guert Gansevoort, was the executive officer of the *Somers* and had presided over the tribunal which found Spencer guilty. Spencer's sympathizers regarded Gansevoort as only a little less to blame than Mackenzie, and Gansevoort seemed more affected by the tribunal's judgment than did Mackenzie. Some critics feel that Melville was prompted to write *Billy Budd* by published accounts of the *Somers* incident. According to biographer Leon Howard, the original of "Billy in the Darbies" was Elisha Small, one of the two sailors executed with Spencer and popular among the *Somers'* crew. Small is reported to have said "God bless the flag" as he was hanged from the yardarm. A little more than two years following the *Somers* incident, the Naval Academy at Annapolis was opened; with its opening came legal safeguards to protect the rights of the enlisted man.

Abraham and Isaac (pp. 77B–78T):

Abraham and Isaac are found in the Bible, the Book of Genesis, Chapter 22. God made a covenant with the patriarch Abraham in which Abraham was to be the father of a multitude of nations. To test Abraham's obedience to Him, God told Abraham to sacrifice the life of his only son, Isaac. Abraham did as God had commanded, but God sent an angel to save the boy at the last moment. Melville recalls the sacrifice of Isaac by Abraham when he conjectures as to what might have passed between Billy and Captain Vere when Vere told Billy of the sentence made by the court. Melville thus conjures up a powerful image of Vere, as the patriarchal father, embracing Billy, as the innocent holocaustal victim.

Elisha (p. 85T):

The reference is more specifically to Elias, who is "the prophet in the chariot disappearing in heaven and dropping his mantle to Elisha. . . ." Both prophets appear in the Bible, the Second Book of Kings, Chapter 2. Elisha is the prophet Eliseus, who received the mantle of the prophet Elias when Elias went up to heaven in a fiery chariot. Elias was the prophet who had denounced King Ahab and his wife Jezebel. Melville spoke of Elias as Elijah in *Moby Dick*. Here the reference to Elias is used poetically to indicate the passing of night into day, like the dropping of Elias' mantle upon Elisha.

Orpheus (p. 90B):

He appears in both Greek and Roman stories as the musician who followed his wife Eurydice into the underworld. He was promised that he might bring her back to the world of the living if he would not look back at her as she followed him. But he could not resist one backward glance and so lost her forever. In Melville's provocative image, Captain Vere reaffirms his allegiance to law. He has just ordered a drumbeat to quarters following Billy's burial to help dissolve the crowd, as he sees the necessity for law to order mankind.

CRITICAL EXCERPTS

Selected from the hundreds of articles, biographies, and volumes of criticism written about Herman Melville, here are some excerpts that should prove challenging.

1. *In the character of Billy Budd, Melville attempts to portray the native purity and nobility of the uncorrupted man. . . . Billy Budd, finished within a few months before the end of Melville's life, would seem to teach that, though the wages of sin is death, sinners and saints alike toil for a common hire. In* Billy Budd *the orphic sententiousness is gone, it is true. But gone also is the brisk lucidity, the sparkle, the verve. Only the disillusion abided with him [Melville] to the last.*

> Herman Melville, Mariner and Mystic, Raymond Weaver, Pageant Books, Inc., first printed in 1921.

2. Billy Budd *is the story of three men in the British Navy: it is also the story of the world, the spirit, and the devil. Melville left a note, crossed out in the original manuscript, "Here ends a story not unwarranted by what happens in this incongruous world of ours—innocence and infirmity, spiritual depravity, and firm respite." The meaning is so obvious that one shrinks from underlining it.*

> Herman Melville, Lewis Mumford, New York Literary Guild of America, 1929.

3. *At last he [Melville] was reconciled. He accepted the situation as a tragic necessity; and to meet that tragedy bravely was to find peace, the ultimate peace of resignation, even in an incongruous world. As Melville's own end approached, he cried out with Billy Budd: "God bless Captain Vere!" In this final affirmation, he died.*

> Herman Melville, Mumford.

4. . . . *the real feeling of* Billy Budd. *This feeling is very
deep and very affecting; it triumphs over the stiff-jointed
prose, the torpidity of the movement, the excess of commentary, and Melville's failure to quicken any of the scenes
with a full dramatic life. In spite of these blemishes of form
and manner, the persons in* Billy Budd *and the moral drama
they enact have too much largeness, as well as too much
subtlety, in their poetic representativeness, not to leave a
permanent stamp on the imagination. For the tale of the
Handsome Sailor and his unhappy end has an archetypal
depth and scope that no reader can quite mistake; it is Melville's version of a primordial fable, the fable of the Fall of
Man, the loss of Paradise.*

> *Herman Melville*, Newton Arvin,
> William Sloane Associates, 1950.

5. *Melville's story has the quality of a Greek myth: it is so
basic and so fertile that it can be retold or dramatized in
various ways.*

> Letter from E. M. Forster, Septem-
> ber 1951.

6. *How odiously Vere comes out in the trial scene! At first
he stays in the witness-box, as he should; then he constitutes
himself both counsel for the prosecution and judge, and never
stops lecturing the court until the boy is sentenced to death.
. . . His unseemly harangue arises, I think, from Melville's
wavering attitude toward an impeccable commander, a superior philosopher, and a British aristocrat. Every now and
then, he doused Billy's light and felt that Vere, being well-
educated and just, must shine like a star.*

> Letter from E. M. Forster.

7. *The most striking of these additions was the elaboration
of Captain Vere's personality until he, rather than Billy
Budd, almost became the central figure of the story.*

> *Herman Melville*, Leon Howard,
> University of California Press,
> 1951.

8. *Despite Melville's eloquence, his humor, his tragic sense of life, his often successful use of myth, symbol, and allegory counterbalanced with a solid realism, his art has distinct limitations. He was not superbly a fictional inventor. Particularly the voyage books, including* Moby Dick, *depend a good deal on Melville's own experiences of knocking around the world as a sailor; and they show a considerable dependence on his reading of books by ship captains and explorers. . . . The contributors to the present volume . . . are content to take him as a writer of romance—that particular kind of poetic fiction which we associate with Cooper, Hawthorne, Poe, Mark Twain, and even a modern writer like Hemingway.*

> Melville, *A Collection of Critical Essays,* Richard Chase, Editor, Prentice-Hall, Inc., 1962.

9. *Some critics have seen a retelling of the story of Christ that constitutes Melville's "testament of acceptance" after all the years of doubt and defiance. Others, interpreting it primarily as satire and irony, have seen a subtle diabolism at work throughout the story. Some have read the story as a commentary on the impersonality and essential brutality of the modern state, exacting death penalties of the innocent. Still others have found the tale an affirmation of the need, even at the risk of injustice, for society to protect itself and to insure order for the general welfare.*

> *A Reader's Guide to Herman Melville,* James E. Miller, Jr., Farrar, Straus, and Cudahy, 1962.

10. *But Billy is much more complex than simply a duplicate of Christ. Christlike, yes, but also like Adam—Adam before the Fall. . . . The main import of this figure is that it emphasizes Billy's ignorance of evil: unlike Christ's, Billy's innocence is compounded, like Adam's before he ate the fruit, of his lack of knowledge of good and evil, and not of a profound insight into the nature of the world and man.*

> *A Reader's Guide to Herman Melville,* Miller.

11. *Claggart is the accomplished hypocrite. . . . Nothing less than "natural depravity" itself is the real motivating force within Claggart. . . . As he lies sprawled under Billy's blow, Claggart's inert body resembles a "dead snake." But the satanic snake is never really dead: Claggart's "soul" has no doubt taken flight to hell, there to join the devil's eternal rebellion.*

> *A Reader's Guide to Herman Melville*, Miller.

12. *As Billy Budd is a man of all heart and no intellect, and John Claggart a man of all intellect and no heart, Captain Vere is the man of moderation with heart and intellect in ideal balance. . . . In all things, that is, Captain Vere avoids exaggerations, extremes. His nickname—Starry Vere—might at first appear ironic to one who, "whatever his sturdy qualities," is "without any brilliant ones." But the stars themselves, unlike the sun, are not flashily brilliant: they are held sturdily fixed in heavenly balance.*

> *A Reader's Guide to Herman Melville*, Miller.

13. Billy Budd *is sufficiently complex to present the many-layered phenomenon which criticism rightly expects in a work of art. . . .* Billy Budd *has been read as a parable of God the Father sacrificing His Son for a fallen world and, alternately, of Pontius Pilate selling out Jesus for present and personal convenience; and finally its sober voice has been taken for a dry mock protesting God and the whole created scheme of things.*

> "The Problem of *Billy Budd*," Edward H. Rosenberry, *Publication of the Modern Language Association*, December 1965.

14. [Billy Budd] *is almost a play, where every word, every accent, every gesture has its part in the narrative weight—as if Melville, too, were atoning, by his perfect craft, for his earlier looseness and carelessness of form, but not indeed*

atoning or repenting for any of his earlier convictions. For just what kind of reconciliation—with God, society or man— did the story describe? The year 1797, to which the action of Billy Budd *belonged, had witnessed all the horrors of the French Revolution, and the subsequent Nore Mutiny in the English navy itself. But Billy, the best sailor on a reputable English merchantman, the "jewel" of the crew, the "peace- maker," the handsome boy, still waves good-by to the* Rights- of-Man *(the name of his ship) when he is conscripted on the high seas for service on the H.M.S.* Indomitable.

Isn't this hero simply Melville's last and farewell portrait of Taipian nature—of the natural man—healthy, open, hand- some, good-humored, generous, confiding, close to the animal level of natural functioning, and quite unaware of sin or evil and all other such civilizational concepts? At least Billy, who soon is called "Baby" Budd and is the favorite among even the hard-bitten sailors of a British man-of-war, has all the pre-Adamic and pre-Edenite virtues. He is "a sort of up- right barbarian," an uncorrupted pagan hero. Like the great heroes of myth, too, he is illegitimate and doesn't know his own parents, who are presumably of noble birth. How Mel- ville stresses "these primitive qualities" in "our Handsome Sailor," and how he creates the illusion in the story of an almost improbable innocence—improbable, that is, to our sophistication. Even Billy's stutter, which according to Mel- ville is designed to make him real, which shows Satan's con- tribution to his angelic constitution—this gift from the "en- vious Marplot of Eden"—is certainly not to be viewed in the Freudian sense of "repressed hostility." Nonsense! If any- thing, it is the mark of animal nature, which doesn't really need speech to express itself, which has not yet reached the level of speech; or of man's higher intelligence, which has brought down upon him all of his civilizational discontents.

But Billy's story is also the parable of innocence without experience or that "defensive ugliness," which Melville noted as being so necessary after the fall of man; or of natural innocence defeated by evil intellect. And here the story swings into a discursive passage on naval history, on Nelson and Trafalgar and the "iron admirals" of the great sailing

ships; on the "proselyting armies" of the French Directory
and their impact on the British sailors; on the secret or care-
fully repressed accounts of the mutinies in the British navy
itself; on all the "glories" of naval war—and all the under-
tones of mass rebellion. These are the two poles of Billy Budd;
and if this divergence is a literary sin, as Melville said, it has
at least "that pleasure which is wickedly said to be in sinning."
The narrative prose of this tale is so dense, so beautiful,
precisely because it is a mixture of history and myth behind
the human drama; not to mention the other levels of radical
social criticism, of philosophy or metaphysics, of cultural and
religious speculation.

Billy is the victim of this historical climate; just as Captain the Honorable Edward Fairfax Vere is the typical product
of such a period. "So it was that for a time on more than one
quarterdeck," Melville added, "anxiety did exist." Starry
Vere's name, given to him by a favorite kinsman, Lord Denton, comes straight out of a seventeenth-century poem by
Andrew Marvell; just as throughout the tale, the Melvillian
wealth of imagery ranges from the pagan myths to Hebrew
scripture to the arrival of the Siamese twins in the United
States—and more, as you will see. What a tremendous
body of knowledge and learning went into this epic of a simple sailor! Now Vere is perhaps one of the best, or most
typical, examples of an honorable English aristocrat doing his
duty to his King, his country and his ship. His opposition to
the French Revolutionary period was not even based on the
fact of his belonging to the "privileged classes," but because
he believed, quite "disinterestedly," that the theories of those
social innovators were "incapable of embodiment in lasting
institutions, and at war with the peace of the world and the
true welfare of mankind."

Captain Vere is an honorable man of law and order. But
the French Revolution had created the same atmosphere of
hysteria in the England of that period as the Russian Revolution did in mid-twentieth-century America.

And what shall we say of the third member of this ill-fated
male trinity on board the H.M.S. Indomitable? Around John
Claggart, master-at-arms, Melville brought together another

fascinating cluster of sea facts—just as Moby Dick *gives the whole economic base of the whaling industry and of the floating whale-oil factories. Was Claggart, who is also compared to the Rev. Dr. Titus Oates, a natural villain with something "defective or abnormal in the constitution and blood"? Was he simply the evil principle in nature itself, compared with Billy's primary and absolute goodness? This would please those critics who see Melville as a native American Dostoevsky in the transcendentalist epoch of universal sweetness and light. And Melville was too much of a realist not to acknowledge that evil shapes and forms exist in nature itself. He was actually our first great and primary realist, as well as our first great naturalist (if we ignore the doctrinaire historians of our literary movements). He was the real link between the transcendentalists and Theodore Dreiser, who in turn, oddly enough, was something of a transcendentalist at heart.*

Melville indeed describes Claggart's "ferreting genius," his "ingratiating deference," his "austere patriotism," or pretense of patriotism, in terms of that "natural depravity" that was recognized both in the Bible and in Plato. This maritime chief of police is among those who have "a mania in the brain or rabies of the heart." He is the serpent in Billy's Edenite garden of life and a brilliant portrait in the story. The discussion of his evil is a marvelous section again of philosophy, metaphysics, religion, social history and economic conditions. And Melville mentions almost every possible reason for Claggart's "unreasoning" hatred of Billy except the one that is so clearly revealed in the narrative itself. That Claggart "might have been" (or actually is) in love with Billy; that he has repressed this passion, being above all a man of "reason"; and that he is insanely jealous of Billy's good looks, good humor and general popularity. But Claggart's hatred is repressed too. He goes about his secret persecution of the Handsome Sailor altogether logically and "reasonably."

Those are the true madmen, according to Melville, who give every appearance of decency, respectability, sobriety, common sense and calm judgment; their emotions being completely controlled by the mind. Yes, Claggart was "the direct reverse of a saint," but also— "To pass from a normal na-

ture to him one must cross 'the deadly space between.' "
*Neither did he typify Melville's view that nature itself was
evil—far from it. Perhaps it was just because he did not
permit his own natural functioning, whatever it was, to operate that he became all repression, all intellect, all evil.
Claggart's depravity partook nothing "of the sordid or sensual," so Melville added, and for such notable instances of
vice, "since these have no vulgar alloy of the brute in them,
but invariably are dominated by intellectuality, one must go
elsewhere. Civilization, especially if of the austerer sort, is
auspicious to it." Now is the argument a little clearer? Claggart is in actuality a later, a final portrait of Ahab and just
as monomaniacal or even more dangerous because his madness
is held under tighter control. And he is pursuing not a whale
but a doe, as it were—and he, in a manner, succeeds. Billy
Budd is all innocent life; and Claggart is again Melville's
concept, not indeed of natural evil, but of the civilized western
man who had been cut off from all the natural impulses, who
has now become an actual criminal.*

*Though space is short, I cannot omit a reference to "the
Dansker" in* Billy Budd—*another of the marvelous pro-
files of seafaring men in the story. There are the meetings
of "the young Achilles" and the "sea Chiron," who knows the
truth of what is happening, but has reached "that bitter
prudence which never interferes in aught and never gives
advice." Then there is the dramatic episode that hinges on
"a man-of-war's-man's spilled soup," that "greasy fluid" that
Claggart believes Billy to have deliberately let drop in his
path. "Passion, and passion in its profoundest, is not a thing
demanding a palatial stage whereon to play its part," said
Melville. "Down among the groundlings, among the beggars
and rakers of the garbage, profound passion is enacted. And
the circumstances that provoke it, however trivial or mean,
are no measure of its power." And wasn't Melville here, quite
like Whitman, sounding the manifesto of the new literature
of democracy? Wasn't he the other prime poet of this new
literature—with his passionate groundlings, his fateful cup of
greasy soup—who in fact prophesied the advent of the American realists and naturalists of the twentieth century?*

*But then the other, the "aristocratic principle" of our native.
literature, so widely acclaimed in the last decade, is probably
confined to only one American fiction-writer—Henry James.
There is the confrontation scene in* Billy Budd *where Claggart
finally traduces the Handsome Sailor to Captain Vere (the
charge is fomenting mutiny and treason) and the skeptical
captain orders Billy to face his enemy. Scenting this mysterious danger, Billy has been behaving, Melville says, "like
a young horse fresh from the pasture suddenly inhaling a vile
whiff from some chemical factory." (And now is it clear
where this artist stood as to nature and society, as to animal
health and social "progress"?) Billy's seaborne innocence has
the fatal lack of the landsman's finesse, we are told in tra-
versing that "oblique, tedious, barren game hardly worth that
poor candle burnt out in playing it." There is also the
"glittering dental satire" of Claggart's, shortly before he repeats the same false accusation to Billy's face, and the sailor,
overcome by anger and despair, unable to speak (his stutter
betrays him), strikes Claggart "full upon the forehead" and
kills him.*

*Billy's reaction is instinctive; and he strikes just at that
"center of reason" that has condemned his primitive virtue
to shame and dishonor. Again Melville repeats this theme
when he remarks that the Handsome Sailor, Baby Budd,
might have posed for "Adam before the fall." This blow upon
the forehead is the response of "betrayed nature," as it were,
to the "superior knowledge" of evil. But why does Captain
Vere suddenly change (like the moon emerging from eclipse
with "another aspect") from a beneficent father-image to the
stern law-giver? He knows that Billy is "right," that Claggart
is a "dead serpent" who has corrupted Adam with false
knowledge; that this is also the "divine judgment on Ananias,"
who lied not to men but to God, and was struck down by an
angel of God. "Yet the angel must hang!"*

*Why? And which God in fact are we dealing with? Does
Vere represent the Hebraic God of justice (also wrath) whose
advent signified the taming of pagan nature? Or is it that dour
and puritanical figurehead of New England's Calvinism for
whom life was only sin and depravity? Or is there still another*

aspect of "God" involved here? Why does Vere change so suddenly; and then demand Billy's punishment so intensely, so relentlessly, when he might have waited to present the case to the admiralty—when his own subordinate officers are reluctant to accede to his command of hanging the Handsome Sailor?

We realize that this honorable sea captain has in turn become obsessed with the necessity of Billy's death; or that he is the "sudden victim of aberration," as the ship's surgeon thinks about Vere's own quest of vengeance and punishment. Is this the treacherous nature of all fathers, as Melville might have opined, and of all father-Gods too, standing so righteously for law and order and all those repressive institutions of society? For there is no doubt that deep within his own heart, Captain Vere is afraid of incipient mutiny on the H.M.S. Indomitable. He, too, represents, at base, the anxiety and the hysteria of his age before the rising tide of revolutionary reforms. Billy must be made an example of the warship's relentless discipline—just or not—but immediately, at once, publicly. The ship's crew, as Vere says, must realize this; or else they might think that authority was indecisive, was trembling. According to "natural justice," Billy is "innocent before God," Vere even declares. But their allegiance is not to nature, but to the King—and the King has declared a state of Martial Law—the law of the Mutiny Act itself.

Thus Billy is the victim not only of the vicious and "rational" Claggart, but of civilized justice too, which includes, which bends down before, the social pressures of the time. Is this the famous Melvillian acquiescence to God and society —the final submission of this rebellious and purehearted spirit to the forces of law, justice, order and "social reality"? (Isn't there also, in this parable of the pagan sailor subjected to such mysterious persecution and sudden death, some identification with Melville himself, some reflection of his own mysteriously thwarted literary career?) No, the acquiescence, the submission, the resignation of the artist in Billy Budd were those only of a Greek tragedy; and if the story's hero goes to his death so stoically, so heroically, to the point of saluting Captain Vere, it is the last mark of Billy's sublime nature, rather than of Melville's approval of Vere's possessed behavior. But Billy,

*as the embodiment of primary and pagan human nature,
had to die before the advance of society and the path of
civilizational "progress." Just as the beautiful, free, joyous
natural society of Typee had to be corrupted and condemned
—and finally obliterated—by the combined force of the whaling ships and the missionaries; by the brute force of eco-
nomics, and the rationalizing facade of religion.*

*There is the ambiguous false ending of Billy Budd, where
Melville does seem to accept the sailor's death, as "the way
things are." But the real moral of the fable comes after and
transcends the pretended moral of mutiny and martial law.
(This story is no Caine Mutiny; just as Typee had a far
different conclusion from that in James Michener's Hawaii.)
There is the sudden ironical reference to the battle lanterns
that hang over Billy's chained, imprisoned and doomed body.
"Fed with the oil supplied by the war-contractors (whose
gains, honest or otherwise, are in every land an anticipated
portion of the harvest of death), with flickering splashes of
dirty yellow light they pollute the pale moonshine . . ." There
is the description of the ship's chaplain endeavoring vainly
to convert Billy's pagan soul. "Not that, like children, Billy
was incapable of conceiving what death really is. No, but he
was wholly without irrational fear of it, a fear more prevalent
in highly civilized communities than those so-called barbarous
ones which in all respects stand nearer to unadulterate nature."*

*"A barbarian Billy radically was," Melville affirmed once
more at the story's end. And a barbarian, in this sense,
Melville remained, without change, without renunciation, without atonement and without compromise, to the end of his
own life. Of course Billy, unlike Melville, listened politely to
the formal theological doctrine of his period. "And this sailor
way of taking clerical discourse is not wholly unlike the way
in which the pioneer of Christianity full of transcendent
miracles was received long ago on tropic isles by any superior
savage so called—a Tahitian, say of Captain Cook's time or
shortly after that time." Yes, that natural paradise of Typee
still bloomed in Melville's memories of life and man. And
then, just what is the purpose of a chaplain aboard a man-
of-war? "Bluntly put, a chaplain is the minister of the Prince*

*of Peace serving in the host of the god of war—Mars. . . .
Why then is he there? Because he indirectly subserves the
purpose attested by the cannon; because, too, he lends the
sanction of the religion of the meek to that which practically
is the abrogation of everything but brute force."*

Was that the end product of the long centuries of man's
heartbreaking struggle for social evolution? Well, at least
Melville still thought so toward the close of the nineteenth
century; and perhaps even more strongly, if more subtly, in
Billy Budd *than in* Moby Dick. *Nowhere had he changed his
earliest, his primary, his deepest convictions as an artist—
those radical convictions that made him the great and original
American artist that he was. Here was the final protest; but
where was that final resignation? Beneath the irony and humor
in the marvelous prose texture of the tale,* Billy Budd *is a
remarkable example of tragic realism; but it was no example
of false resignation to the ways of the world, or of Melville's
moral conversion, or his recanting. He was no Claggart, no
false informer as to the real conditions of man's life and
destiny.*

There is that final brilliant touch in Billy Budd *of the
British navy's official account of the Handsome Sailor's death.
(So much for the free press.) The royal British blue-jackets
had another version of the affair in which Baby Budd was the
lamb of God, the scapegoat upon whose beautiful pagan head
(and broken neck) were vented all the discontents of civilization, in its martial phase.*

A note on method: This "new," or at least different, approach, as I believe, to *Billy Budd* is based on a fusion of
Freudian and Reichian concepts of culture and personality,
plus the cultural critique of Otto Rank, as recently projected
and developed by our own brilliant young psycho-cultural
historian and critic, Jack Jones. That Melville's work con-
tained such psychological and civilizational insights, quite
intuitively and altogether prophetically, is nothing new, of
course, in the chronicle of major artists.

"Introduction" to *Billy Budd,* Maxwell Geismar, Washington Square
Press, 1966.

"Say what?" demanded Billy.

"Why, *Jemmy Legs* is *down* on you."

"And what" rejoined Billy in amazement, "has *Jemmy Legs* to do with that cracked afterguardsman?"

"Ho, it was an afterguardsman then. A cat's-paw, a cat's-paw!" And with that exclamation, which, whether it had reference to a light puff of air just then coming over the calm sea, or subtler relation to the afterguardsman, there is no telling, the old Merlin gave a twisting wrench with his black teeth at his plug of tobacco, vouchsafing no reply to Billy's impetuous question, though now repeated, for it was his wont to relapse into grim silence when interrogated in skeptical sort as to any of his sententious oracles, not always very clear ones, rather partaking of that obscurity which invests most Delphic deliverances from any quarter.

Long experience had very likely brought this old man to that bitter prudence which never interferes in aught and never gives advice.

XVII

YES, DESPITE THE DANSKER'S pithy insistence as to the master-at-arms being at the bottom of these strange experiences of Billy on board the *Indomitable,* the young sailor was ready to ascribe them to almost anybody but the man who, to use Billy's own expression, "always had a pleasant word for him." This is to be wondered at. Yet not so much to be wondered at. In certain matters, some sailors even in mature life remain unsophisticated enough. But a young seafarer of the disposition of our athletic foretopman, is much of a child-man. And yet a child's utter innocence is but its blank ignorance, and the innocence more or less wanes as intelligence waxes. But in Billy Budd intelligence, such as it was, had advanced, while yet his simple-mindedness remained for the most part unaffected. Experience is a teacher indeed; yet did Billy's years make his experience small. Besides, he had none of that intuitive knowledge of the bad which in natures not good or incompletely so foreruns experience, and therefore may pertain, as in some instances it too clearly does pertain, even to youth.

And what could Billy know of man except of man as a mere sailor? And the old-fashioned sailor, the veritable man-before-the-mast, the sailor from boyhood up, he, though indeed of the same species as a landsman is in some respects singularly distinct from him. The sailor is frankness, the landsman is finesse. Life is not a game with the sailor, demanding the long head; no intricate game of chess where few moves are made in straightforwardness, and ends are attained by indirection; an oblique, tedious, barren game hardly worth that poor candle burnt out in playing it.[8]

Yes, as a class, sailors are in character a juvenile race. Even deviations are marked by juvenility. And this more especially holding true with the sailors of Billy's time. Then, too, certain things which apply to all sailors, do more pointedly operate here and there, upon the junior one. Every sailor, too, is accustomed to obey orders without debating them; his life afloat is externally ruled for him; he is not brought into that promiscuous commerce with mankind where unobstructed free agency on equal terms—equal superficially, at least—soon teaches one that unless upon occasion he exercise a distrust keen in proportion to the fairness of the appearance, some foul turn may be served him. A ruled undemonstrative distrustfulness is so habitual, not with businessmen so much, as with men who know their kind in less shallow relations than business, namely, certain men-of-the-world; and that they come at last to employ it all but unconsciously; and some of them would very likely feel real surprise at being charged with it as one of their general characteristics.

---

8 *Cf.* Shakespeare, *Macbeth*, Act V, Scene 5, ll. 15–17.

XVIII

BUT AFTER THE LITTLE matter at the mess Billy Budd no
more found himself in strange trouble at times about his
hammock or his clothes bag or what not. While, as to that
smile that occasionally sunned him, and the pleasant passing
word, these were if not more frequent, yet if anything more
pronounced than before.

But for all that, there were certain other demonstrations
now. When Claggart's unobserved glance happened to light
on belted Billy rolling along the upper gundeck in the leisure
of the second dogwatch exchanging passing broadsides of fun
with other young promenaders in the crowd; that glance would
follow the cheerful sea Hyperion[9] with a settled meditative
and melancholy expression, his eyes strangely suffused with
incipient feverish tears. Then would Claggart look like the
man of sorrows. Yes, and sometimes the melancholy expression would have in it a touch of soft yearning, as if Claggart
could even have loved Billy but for fate and ban. But this
was an evanescence, and quickly repented of, as it were, by
an immitigable look, pinching and shriveling the visage into
the momentary semblance of a wrinkled walnut. But sometimes catching sight in advance of the foretopman coming in
his direction, he would, upon their nearing, step aside a little
to let him pass, dwelling upon Billy for the moment with the
glittering dental satire of a Guise.[1] But upon any abrupt
unforeseen encounter a red light would flash forth from his
eye like a spark from an anvil in a dusk smithy. That quick
fierce light was a strange one, darted from orbs which in

9 In early Greek myth, the Titan Helios, god of the sun; later identified with
Apollo, god of manly youth and beauty.

1 The Guises, a powerful ducal family of France in the sixteenth and seventeenth centuries, engaged in violent intrigues attractive to romancers, for example Dumas. As for the "glittering dental satire," *cf.* Hamlet's discovery
"that one may smile . . . and be a villain" (Act I, Scene 5, ll. 103–105).

repose were of a color nearest approaching a deeper violet, the softest of shades.

Though some of these caprices of the pit could not but be observed by their object, yet were they beyond the construing of such a nature. And the *thews* of Billy were hardly compatible with that sort of sensitive spiritual organization which in some cases instinctively conveys to ignorant innocence an admonition of the proximity of the malign. He thought the master-at-arms acted in a manner rather queer at times. That was all. But the occasional frank air and pleasant word went for what they purported to be, the young sailor never having heard as yet of the "too fair-spoken man."

Had the foretopman been conscious of having done or said anything to provoke the ill will of the official, it would have been different with him, and his sight might have been purged if not sharpened. As it was, innocence was his blinder.

So was it with him in yet another matter. Two minor officers—the armorer and captain of the hold, with whom he had never exchanged a word, his position in the ship not bringing him into contact with them; these men now for the first began to cast upon Billy when they chanced to encounter him, that peculiar glance which evidences that the man from whom it comes has been some way tampered with and to the prejudice of him upon whom the glance lights. Never did it occur to Billy as a thing to be noted or a thing suspicious, though he well knew the fact, that the armorer and captain of the hold, with the ship's-yeoman, apothecary, and others of that grade, were by naval usage, messmates of the master-at-arms, men with ears convenient to his confidential tongue.

But the general popularity that our Handsome Sailor's manly forwardness upon occasion, and his irresistible good nature, indicating no mental superiority tending to excite an invidious feeling; this good will on the part of most of his shipmates made him the less to concern himself about such mute aspects toward him as those whereto allusion has just been made.

As to the afterguardsman, though Billy for reasons already given necessarily saw little of him, yet when the two did happen to meet, invariably came the fellow's offhand cheerful recognition, sometimes accompanied by a passing pleasant word or two. Whatever that equivocal young person's original design may really have been, or the design of which he might have been the deputy, certain it was from his manner upon these occasions, that he had wholly dropped it.

It was as if his precocity of crookedness (and every vulgar villain is precocious) had for once deceived him, and the man he had sought to entrap as a simpleton had, through his very simplicity ignorantly baffled him.

But shrewd ones may opine that it was hardly possible for Billy to refrain from going up to the afterguardsman and bluntly demanding to know his purpose in the initial interview, so abruptly closed in the forechains. Shrewd ones may also think it but natural in Billy to set about sounding some of the other impressed men of the ship in order to discover what basis, if any, there was for the emissary's obscure suggestions as to plotting disaffection aboard. Yes, the shrewd may so think. But something more, or rather, something else than mere shrewdness is perhaps needful for the due understanding of such a character as Billy Budd's.

As to Claggart, the monomania in the man—if that indeed it were—as involuntarily disclosed by starts in the manifestations detailed, yet in general covered over by his self-contained and rational demeanor; this, like a subterranean fire, was eating its way deeper and deeper in him. Something decisive must come of it.

XIX

AFTER THE MYSTERIOUS interview in the forechains, the one so abruptly ended there by Billy, nothing especially German[2] to the story occurred until the events now about to be narrated.

Elsewhere it has been said that in the lack of frigates (of course better sailers than line-of-battle ships) in the English squadron up the Straits at that period, the *Indomitable* was

---

2 Cf. "germane," meaning "akin."

occasionally employed not only as an available substitute for a scout, but at times on detached service of more important kind. This was not alone because of her sailing qualities, not common in a ship of her rate, but quite as much, probably, that the character of her commander, it was thought, specially adapted him for any duty where under unforeseen difficulties a prompt initiative might have to be taken in some matter demanding knowledge and ability in addition to those qualities implied in good seamanship. It was on an expedition of the latter sort, a somewhat distant one, and when the *Indomitable* was almost at her furthest remove from the fleet that in the latter part of an afternoon watch she unexpectedly came in sight of a ship of the enemy. It proved to be a frigate. The latter perceiving through the glass that the weight of men and metal would be heavily against her, invoking her light heels crowded sail to get away. After a chase urged almost against hope and lasting until about the middle of the first dogwatch, she signally succeeded in effecting her escape.

Not long after the pursuit had been given up, and ere the excitement incident thereto had altogether waned away, the master-at-arms ascending from his cavernous sphere made his appearance cap in hand by the mainmast respectfully waiting the notice of Captain Vere then solitary walking the weather side of the quarterdeck, doubtless somewhat chafed at the failure of the pursuit. The spot where Claggart stood was the place allotted to men of lesser grades seeking some more particular interview either with the officer-of-the-deck or the captain himself. But from the latter it was not often that a sailor or petty-officer of those days would seek a hearing; only some exceptional cause, would, according to established custom, have warranted that.

Presently, just as the commander absorbed in his reflections was on the point of turning aft in his promenade, he became sensible of Claggart's presence, and saw the doffed cap held in deferential expectancy. Here be it said that Captain Vere's personal knowledge of this petty-officer had only begun at the time of the ship's last sailing from home, Claggart then for the first, in transfer from a ship detained for repairs, supplying on board the *Indomitable* the place of a previous master-at-arms disabled and ashore.

No sooner did the commander observe who it was that now deferentially stood awaiting his notice, than a peculiar expression came over him. It was not unlike that which uncontrollably will flit across the countenance of one at unawares encountering a person who though known to him indeed has hardly been long enough known for thorough knowledge, but something in whose aspect nevertheless now for the first provokes a vaguely repellent distaste. But coming to a stand, and resuming much of his wonted official manner, save that a sort of impatience lurked in the intonation of the opening word, he said "Well? What is it, Master-at-Arms?"

With the air of a subordinate grieved at the necessity of being a messenger of ill tidings, and while conscientiously determined to be frank, yet equally resolved upon shunning overstatement, Claggart at this invitation or rather summons to disburden, spoke up. What he said, conveyed in the language of no uneducated man, was to the effect following if not altogether in these words, namely, that during the chase and preparations for the possible encounter he had seen enough to convince him that at least one sailor aboard was a dangerous character in a ship mustering some who not only had taken a guilty part in the late serious troubles, but others also who, like the man in question, had entered His Majesty's service under another form than enlistment.

At this point Captain Vere with some impatience, interrupted him: "Be direct, man; say impressed men."

Claggart made a gesture of subservience, and proceeded. Quite lately he (Claggart) had begun to suspect that on the gundecks some sort of movement prompted by the sailor in question was covertly going on, but he had not thought himself warranted in reporting the suspicion so long as it remained indistinct. But from what he had that afternoon observed in the man referred to the suspicion of something clandestine going on had advanced to a point less removed from certainty. He deeply felt, he added, the serious responsibility assumed in making a report involving such possible

consequences to the individual mainly concerned, besides tending to augment those natural anxieties which every naval commander must feel in view of extraordinary outbreaks so recent as those which, he sorrowfully said it, it needed not to
name.

Now at the first broaching of the matter Captain Vere,
taken by surprise, could not wholly dissemble his disquietude.
But as Claggart went on, the former's aspect changed into
restiveness under something in the witness' manner in giving
his testimony. However, he refrained from interrupting him.
And Claggart, continuing, concluded with this:

"God forbid, your honor, that the *Indomitable's* should be
the experience of the——"

"Never mind that!" here peremptorily broke in the superior,
his face altering with anger, instinctively divining the ship that
the other was about to name, one in which the Nore Mutiny
had assumed a singularly tragical character that for a time
jeopardized the life of its commander. Under the circumstances he was indignant at the purposed allusion. When the
commissioned officers themselves were on all occasions very
heedful how they referred to the recent events, for a petty-
officer unnecessarily to allude to them in the presence of his
captain, this struck him as a most immodest presumption. Besides, to his quick sense of self-respect, it even looked under
the circumstances something like an attempt to alarm him.
Nor at first was he without some surprise that one who so far
as he had hitherto come under his notice had shown considerable tact in his function should in this particular evince
such lack of it.

But these thoughts and kindred dubious ones flitting across
his mind were suddenly replaced by an intuitional surmise
which though as yet obscure in form served practically to
affect his reception of the ill tidings. Certain it is, that long
versed in everything pertaining to the complicated gundeck
life, which like every other form of life, has its secret mines
and dubious side, the side popularly disclaimed, Captain Vere
did not permit himself to be unduly disturbed by the general
tenor of his subordinate's report. Furthermore, if in view of

recent events prompt action should be taken at the first palpable sign of recurring insubordination, for all that, not judicious would it be, he thought, to keep the idea of lingering disaffection alive by undue forwardness in crediting an informer even if his own subordinate and charged among other things with police surveillance of the crew. This feeling would not perhaps have so prevailed with him were it not that upon a prior occasion the patriotic zeal officially evinced by Claggart had somewhat irritated him as appearing rather supersensible and strained. Furthermore, something even in the official's self-possessed and somewhat ostentatious manner in making his specifications strangely reminded him of a bandsman, perjurous witness in a capital case before a court-martial ashore of which, when a lieutenant, he Captain Vere had been a member.

Now the peremptory check given to Claggart in the matter of the arrested allusion was quickly followed up by this: "You say that there is at least one dangerous man aboard. Name him."

"William Budd. A foretopman, your honor—"

"William Budd" repeated Captain Vere with unfeigned astonishment, "and mean you the man that Lieutenant Ratcliffe took from the merchantman not very long ago—the young fellow who seems to be so popular with the men—Billy, the Handsome Sailor, as they call him?"

"The same, your honor; but for all his youth and good looks, a deep one. Not for nothing does he insinuate himself into the good will of his shipmates, since at the least all hands will at a pinch say a good word for him at all hazards. Did Lieutenant Ratcliffe happen to tell your honor of that adroit fling of Budd's, jumping up in the cutter's bow under the merchantman's stern when he was being taken off? It is even masked by that sort of good-humored air that at heart he resents his impressment. You have but noted his fair cheek. A man-trap may be under his ruddy-tipped daisies."

Now the Handsome Sailor as a signal figure among the crew had naturally enough attracted the Captain's attention from the first. Though in general not very demonstrative to

his officers, he had congratulated Lieutenant Ratcliffe upon
his good fortune in lighting on such a fine specimen of the
genus homo, who in the nude might have posed for a statue
of young Adam before the Fall.

As to Billy's adieu to the ship *Rights-of-Man,* which the
boarding lieutenant had indeed reported to him but in a deferential way more as a good story than aught else, Captain
Vere, though mistakenly understanding it as a satiric sally,
had but thought so much the better of the impressed man
for it; as a military sailor, admiring the spirit that could take
an arbitrary enlistment so merrily and sensibly. The foretopman's conduct, too, so far as it had fallen under the captain's notice had confirmed the first happy augury, while the
new recruit's qualities as a *sailor-man* seemed to be such that
he had thought of recommending him to the executive officer
for promotion to a place that would more frequently bring
him under his own observation, namely, the captaincy of the
mizzen-top, replacing there in the starboard watch a man not
so young whom partly for that reason he deemed less fitted
for the post. Be it parenthesized here that since the mizzen-
top-men having not to handle such breadths of heavy canvas
as the lower sails on the mainmast and foremast, a young
man if of the right stuff not only seems best adapted to duty
there, but in fact is generally selected for the captaincy of
that top, and the company under him are light hands and often
but striplings. In sum, Captain Vere had from the beginning
deemed Billy Budd to be what in the naval parlance of the
time was called a *"King's bargain,"* that is to say, for His
Britannic Majesty's navy a capital investment at small outlay
or none at all.

After a brief pause during which the reminiscences above
mentioned passed vividly through his mind and he weighed
the import of Claggart's last suggestion conveyed in the phrase
"pitfall under the clover,"[3] and the more he weighed it the

3 *Cf.* "A man-trap . . . under his . . . daisies," ending the third paragraph
above. There Melville had first written, then canceled, "a pitfall under his ruddy
clover," the words that Captain Vere remembers here. The discrepancy
might have been corrected had Melville seen the manuscript through press.

less reliance he felt in the informer's good faith. Suddenly he turned upon him and in a low voice: "Do you come to me, Master-at-Arms, with so foggy a tale? As to Budd, cite me an act or spoken word of his confirmatory of what you in general charge against him. Stay," drawing nearer to him, "heed what you speak. Just now, and in a case like this, there is a yardarm end for the false witness."

"Ah, your honor!" sighed Claggart mildly shaking his shapely head as in sad deprecation of such unmerited severity of tone. Then, bridling—erecting himself as in virtuous self-assertion, he circumstantially alleged certain words and acts, which collectively, if credited, led to presumptions mortally inculpating Budd. And for some of these averments, he added, substantiating proof was not far.

With gray eyes impatient and distrustful essaying to fathom to the bottom Claggart's calm violet ones, Captain Vere again heard him out; then for the moment stood ruminating. The mood he evinced, Claggart—himself for the time liberated from the other's scrutiny—steadily regarded with a look difficult to render—a look curious of the operation of his tactics, a look such as might have been that of the spokesman of the envious children of Jacob deceptively imposing upon the troubled patriarch the blood-dyed coat of young Joseph.

Though something exceptional in the moral quality of Captain Vere made him, in earnest encounter with a fellowman, a veritable touchstone of that man's essential nature, yet now as to Claggart and what was really going on in him his feeling partook less of intuitional conviction than of strong suspicion clogged by strange dubieties. The perplexity he evinced proceeded less from aught touching the man informed against— as Claggart doubtless opined—than from considerations how best to act in regard to the informer. At first indeed he was naturally for summoning that substantiation of his allegations which Claggart said was at hand. But such a proceeding would result in the matter at once getting abroad, which in the present stage of it, he thought, might undesirably affect the ship's company. If Claggart was a false witness—that closed the affair. And therefore before trying the accusation, he would first practically test the accuser; and he thought this could be done in a quiet undemonstrative way.

The measure he determined upon involved a shifting of the scene, a transfer to a place less exposed to observation than the broad quarterdeck. For although the few gun room officers there at the time had, in due observance of naval etiquette, withdrawn to leeward the moment Captain Vere had begun his promenade on the deck's weather side; and though during the colloquy with Claggart they of course ventured not to diminish the distance; and though throughout the interview Captain Vere's voice was far from high, and Claggart's silvery and low; and the wind in the cordage and the wash of the sea helped the more to put them beyond earshot; nevertheless, the interview's continuance already had attracted observation from some topmen aloft and other sailors in the waist or further forward.

Having determined upon his measures, Captain Vere forthwith took action. Abruptly turning to Claggart he asked, "Master-at-Arms, is it now Budd's watch aloft?"

"No, your honor." Whereupon, "Mr. Wilkes!" summoning the nearest midshipman, "tell Albert to come to me." Albert was the captain's hammock boy, a sort of sea valet in whose discretion and fidelity his master had much confidence. The lad appeared. "You know Budd the foretopman?"

"I do, sir."

"Go find him. It is his watch off. Manage to tell him out of earshot that he is wanted aft. Contrive it that he speaks to nobody. Keep him in talk yourself. And not till you get well aft here, not till then let him know that the place where he is wanted is my cabin. You understand. Go.—Master-at-Arms, show yourself on the decks below, and when you think it time for Albert to be coming with his man, stand by quietly to follow the sailor in."

Now WHEN THE FORETOPMAN found himself closeted there, as it were, in the cabin with the captain and Claggart, he was surprised enough. But it was a surprise unaccompanied by apprehension or distrust. To an immature nature essentially honest and humane, forewarning intimations of subtler danger from one's kind come tardily if at all. The only thing that took shape in the young sailor's mind was this: Yes, the captain, I have always thought, looks kindly upon me. Wonder if he's going to make me his coxswain. I should like that. And maybe now he is going to ask the master-at-arms about me.

"Shut the door there, sentry," said the commander. "Stand without, and let nobody come in.—Now, Master-at-Arms, tell this man to his face what you told of him to me," and stood prepared to scrutinize the mutually confronting visages.

With the measured step and calm collected air of an asylum physician approaching in the public hall some patient beginning to show indications of a coming paroxysm, Claggart deliberately advanced within short range of Billy, and mesmerically looking him in the eye, briefly recapitulated the accusation.

Not at first did Billy take it in. When he did, the rose-tan of his cheek looked struck as by white leprosy. He stood like one impaled and gagged. Meanwhile the accuser's eyes removing not as yet from the blue dilated ones, underwent a phenomenal change, their wonted rich violet color blurring into a muddy purple. Those lights of human intelligence losing human expression, gelidly protruding like the alien eyes of certain uncatalogued creatures of the deep. The first mesmeric glance was one of serpent fascination; the last was as the hungry lurch of the torpedo fish.

"Speak, man!" said Captain Vere to the transfixed one struck by his aspect even more than by Claggart's. "Speak! defend yourself." Which appeal caused but a strange dumb gesturing and gurgling in Billy; amazement at such an accusation so suddenly sprung on inexperienced nonage; this, and, it may be horror of the accuser, serving to bring out his lurking defect and in this instance for the time intensifying it into a convulsed tongue-tie; while the intent head and entire form straining forward in an agony of ineffectual eagerness to obey the injunction to speak and defend himself, gave an expression to the face like that of a condemned vestal priestess in the moment of being buried alive, and in the first struggle against suffocation.

Though at the time Captain Vere was quite ignorant of Billy's liability to vocal impediment, he now immediately divined it, since vividly Billy's aspect recalled to him that of a bright young schoolmate of his whom he had once seen struck by much the same startling impotence in the act of eagerly rising in the class to be foremost in response to a testing question put to it by the master. Going close up to the young sailor, and laying a soothing hand on his shoulder, he said: "There is no hurry, my boy. Take your time, take your time." Contrary to the effect intended, these words so fatherly in tone, doubtless touching Billy's heart to the quick, prompted yet more violent efforts at utterance—efforts ending for the time in confirming the paralysis, and bringing to his face an expression which was as a crucifixion to behold. The next instant, quick as the flame from a discharged cannon at night, his right arm shot out, and Claggart dropped to the deck. Whether intentionally or but owing to the young athlete's superior height, the blow had taken effect full upon the forehead, so shapely and intellectual-looking a feature in the master-at-arms; so that the body fell over lengthwise, like a heavy plank tilted from erectness. A gasp or two, and he lay motionless.

"Fated boy," breathed Captain Vere in tone so low as to be almost a whisper, "what have you done! But here, help me."

The twain raised the felled one from the loins up into a sitting position. The spare form flexibly acquiesced, but inertly. It was like handling a dead snake. They lowered it back. Regaining erectness Captain Vere with one hand covering his face stood to all appearance as impassive as the object at his feet. Was he absorbed in taking in all the bearings of the event and what was best not only now at once to be done, but also in the sequel? Slowly he uncovered his face; and the effect was as if the moon emerging from eclipse should reappear with quite another aspect than that which had gone into hiding. The father in him, manifested toward Billy thus far in the scene, was replaced by the military disciplinarian. In his official tone he bade the foretopman retire to a stateroom aft, (pointing it out) and there remain till thence summoned. This order Billy in silence mechanically obeyed. Then going to the cabin door where it opened on the quarterdeck, Captain Vere said to the sentry without, "Tell somebody to send Albert here." When the lad appeared his master so contrived it that he should not catch sight of the prone one. "Albert," he said to him, "tell the surgeon I wish to see him. You need not come back till called." When the surgeon entered—a self-poised character of that grave sense and experience that hardly anything could take him aback—Captain Vere, advanced to meet him, thus unconsciously intercepting his view of Claggart and interrupting the other's wonted ceremonious salutation, and said, "Nay, tell me how it is with yonder man," directing his attention to the prostrate one.

The surgeon looked, and for all his self-command, somewhat started at the abrupt revelation. On Claggart's always pallid complexion, thick black blood was now oozing from nostril and ear. To the gazer's professional eye it was unmistakably no living man that he saw.

"Is it so then?" said Captain Vere intently watching him. "I thought it. But verify it." Whereupon the customary tests confirmed the surgeon's first glance, who now looking up in unfeigned concern, cast a look of intense inquisitiveness upon his superior. But Captain Vere, with one hand to his brow, was standing motionless. Suddenly, catching the surgeon's arm convulsively, he exclaimed pointing down to the body—"It is the divine judgment on Ananias![4] Look!"

4 Having lied, "not . . . unto men, but unto God," Ananias was stricken dead (Acts v: 1–5).

Disturbed by the excited manner he had never before observed in the *Indomitable's* captain, and as yet wholly ignorant
of the affair, the prudent surgeon nevertheless held his peace,
only again looking an earnest interrogation as to what it was
that had resulted in such a tragedy.

But Captain Vere was now again motionless standing absorbed in thought. But again starting, he vehemently exclaimed—"Struck dead by an angel of God! Yet the angel
must hang!"

At these passionate interjections, mere incoherences to the
listener as yet unapprised of the antecedents, the surgeon was
profoundly discomposed. But now as recollecting himself,
Captain Vere in less harsh tone briefly related the circumstances leading up to the event.

"But come; we must dispatch," he added. "Help me to remove him (meaning the body) to yonder compartment,"
designating one opposite that where the foretopman remained
immured. Anew disturbed by a request that as implying a
desire for secrecy, seemed unaccountably strange to him, there
was nothing for the subordinate to do but comply.

"Go now," said Captain Vere with something of his wonted
manner—"Go now. I shall presently call a drum-head court.
Tell the lieutenants what has happened, and tell Mr. Mor-
dant," meaning the captain of marines, "and charge them to
keep the matter to themselves."

XXI

FULL OF DISQUIETUDE and misgiving the surgeon left the cabin.
Was Captain Vere suddenly affected in his mind, or was it but
a transient excitement, brought about by so strange and extraordinary a happening? As to the drum-head court, it struck
the surgeon as impolitic, if nothing more. The thing to do,
he thought, was to place Billy Budd in confinement and in a
way dictated by usage, and postpone further action in so extraordinary a case, to such time as they should rejoin the

squadron, and then refer it to the admiral. He recalled the unwonted agitation of Captain Vere and his excited exclamations so at variance with his normal manner. Was he unhinged? But assuming that he is, it is not so susceptible of proof. What then can he do? No more trying situation is conceivable than that of an officer subordinate under a captain whom he suspects to be, not mad indeed, but yet not quite unaffected in his intellect. To argue his order to him would be insolence. To resist him would be mutiny.

In obedience to Captain Vere he communicated what had happened to the lieutenants and captain of marines, saying nothing as to the captain's state. They fully shared his own surprise and concern. Like him too they seemed to think that such a matter should be referred to the admiral.

XXII

WHO IN THE RAINBOW can draw the line where the violet tint ends and the orange tint begins? Distinctly we see the difference of the colors, but where exactly does the one first blendingly enter into the other? So with sanity and insanity. In pronounced cases there is no question about them. But in some supposed cases, in various degrees supposedly less pronounced, to draw the exact line of demarkation few will undertake though for a fee some professional experts will. There is nothing namable but that some men will undertake to do it for pay.

Whether Captain Vere, as a surgeon professionally and privately surmised, was really the sudden victim of any degree of aberration, one must determine for himself by such light as this narrative may afford.

That the unhappy event which has been narrated could not have happened at a worse juncture was but too true. For it was close on the heel of the suppressed insurrections, an aftertime very critical to naval authority, demanding from every English sea commander two qualities not readily interfusable

—prudence and rigor. Moreover there was something crucial in the case.

In the jugglery of circumstances preceding and attending the event on board the *Indomitable* and in the light of that martial code whereby it was formally to be judged, innocence and guilt personified in Claggart and Budd in effect changed places. In a legal view the apparent victim of the tragedy was he who had sought to victimize a man blameless; and the indisputable deed of the latter, navally regarded, constituted the most heinous of military crimes. Yet more. The essential right and wrong involved in the matter, the clearer that might be, so much the worse for the responsibility of a loyal sea commander inasmuch as he was not authorized to determine the matter on that primitive basis.

Small wonder then that the *Indomitable's* captain though in general a man of rapid decision, felt that circumspectness not less than promptitude was necessary. Until he could decide upon his course, and in each detail; and not only so, but until the concluding measure was upon the point of being enacted, he deemed it advisable, in view of all the circumstances to guard as much as possible against publicity. Here he may or may not have erred. Certain it is however that subsequently in the confidential talk of more than one or two gun rooms and cabins he was not a little criticized by some officers, a fact imputed by his friends and vehemently by his cousin Jack Denton to professional jealousy of Starry Vere. Some imaginative ground for invidious comment there was. The maintenance of secrecy in the matter, the confining all knowledge of it for a time to the place where the homicide occurred, the quarterdeck cabin; in these particulars lurked some resemblance to the policy adopted in those tragedies of the palace which have occurred more than once in the capital founded by Peter the Barbarian.[5]

The case indeed was such that fain would the *Indomitable's* captain have deferred taking any action whatever respecting

5 Peter I, Czar of Russia (1682–1725), called Peter the Great, founded the new Russian capital of St. Petersburg (1703).

it further than to keep the foretopman a close prisoner till the ship rejoined the squadron and then submitting the matter to the judgement of his admiral.

But a true military officer is one particular like a true monk. Not with more of self-abnegation will the latter keep his vows of monastic obedience than the former his vows of allegiance to martial duty.

Feeling that unless quick action was taken on it, the deed of the foretopman, so soon as it should be known on the gun-decks would tend to awaken any slumbering embers of the Nore among the crew, a sense of the urgency of the case overruled in Captain Vere every other consideration. But though a conscientious disciplinarian he was no lover of authority for mere authority's sake. Very far was he from embracing opportunities for monopolizing to himself the perils of moral responsibility, none at least that could properly be referred to an official superior or shared with him by his official equals or even subordinates. So thinking, he was glad it would not be at variance with usage to turn the matter over to a summary court of his own officers, reserving to himself as the one on whom the ultimate accountability would rest, the right of maintaining a supervision of it, or formally or informally interposing at need. Accordingly a drum-head court was summarily convened, he electing the individuals composing it, the first lieutenant, the captain of marines, and the sailing master.

In associating an officer of marines with the sea lieutenants in a case having to do with a sailor the commander perhaps deviated from general custom. He was prompted thereto by the circumstance that he took that soldier to be a judicious person, thoughtful, and not altogether incapable of grappling with a difficult case unprecedented in his prior experience. Yet even as to him he was not without some latent misgiving, for withal he was an extremely good-natured man, an enjoyer of his dinner, a sound sleeper, and inclined to obesity. A man who though he would always maintain his manhood in battle might not prove altogether reliable in a moral dilemma involving aught of the tragic. As to the first lieutenant and the sailing master, Captain Vere could not but be aware that though honest natures, of approved gallantry upon occasion, their intelligence was mostly confined to the matter of active seamanship and the fighting demands of their profession. The court was held in the same cabin where the unfortunate affair had taken place. This cabin, the commander's, embraced the entire area under the poopdeck. Aft, and on either side, was a small stateroom; the one room temporarily a jail and the other a dead-house, and a yet smaller compartment leaving a space between, expanding forward into a goodly oblong of length coinciding with the ship's beam. A skylight of moderate dimension was overhead and at each end of the oblong space were two sashed porthole windows easily convertible back into embrasures for short carronades.

All being quickly in readiness, Billy Budd was arraigned, Captain Vere necessarily appearing as the sole witness in the case, and as such temporarily sinking his rank, though singularly maintaining it in a matter apparently trivial, namely, that he testified from the ship's weather side, with that object having caused the court to sit on the lee side. Concisely he narrated all that had led up to the catastrophe, omitting nothing in Claggart's accusation and deposing as to the manner in which the prisoner had received it. At this testimony the three officers glanced with no little surprise at Billy Budd, the last man they would have suspected either of the mutinous design alleged by Claggart or the undeniable deed he himself had done.

The first lieutenant, taking judicial primacy and turning toward the prisoner, said, "Captain Vere has spoken. Is it or is it not as Captain Vere says?" In response came syllables not so much impeded in the utterance as might have been anticipated. They were these: "Captain Vere tells the truth. It is just as Captain Vere says, but it is not as the master-at-arms said. I have eaten the King's bread and I am true to the King."

"I believe you, my man" said the witness, his voice indicating a suppressed emotion not otherwise betrayed.

"God will bless you for that, Your Honor!" not without stammering said Billy, and all but broke down. But immediately was recalled to self-control by another question, to which with the same emotional difficulty of utterance he said, "No, there was no malice between us. I never bore malice against the master-at-arms. I am sorry that he is dead. I did not mean to kill him. Could I have used my tongue I would not have struck him. But he foully lied to my face and in presence of my captain, and I had to say something, and I could only say it with a blow, God help me!"

In the impulsive above-board manner of the frank one, the court saw confirmed all that was implied in words that just previously had perplexed them, coming as they did from the testifier to the tragedy and promptly following Billy's impassioned disclaimer of mutinous intent—Captain Vere's words, "I believe you, my man."

Next it was asked of him whether he knew of or suspected aught savoring of incipient trouble (meaning mutiny, though the explicit term was avoided) going on in any section of the ship's company.

The reply lingered. This was naturally imputed by the court to the same vocal embarrassment which had retarded or obstructed previous answers. But in main it was otherwise here; the question immediately recalling to Billy's mind the interview with the afterguardsman in the forechains. But an innate repugnance to playing a part at all approaching that of an informer against one's own shipmates—the same erring sense of uninstructed honor which had stood in the way of his reporting the matter at the time though as a loyal man-of-war-man it was incumbent on him, and failure so to do if charged against him and proven, would have subjected him to the heaviest of penalties; this, with the blind feeling now his, that nothing really was being hatched, prevailed with him. When the answer came it was a negative.

"One question more," said the officer of marines now first speaking and with a troubled earnestness. "You tell us that what the master-at-arms said against you was a lie. Now why should he have so lied, so maliciously lied, since you declare there was no malice between you?"

At that question unintentionally touching on a spiritual

sphere wholly obscure to Billy's thoughts, he was nonplussed, evincing a confusion indeed that some observers, such as can readily be imagined, would have construed into involuntary evidence of hidden guilt. Nevertheless he strove some way to answer, but all at once relinquished the vain endeavor, at the same time turning an appealing glance towards Captain Vere as deeming him his best helper and friend. Captain Vere who had been seated for a time rose to his feet, addressing the interrogator. "The question you put to him comes naturally enough. But how can he rightly answer it? or anybody else? unless indeed it be he who lies within there," designating the compartment where lay the corpse. "But the prone one there will not rise to our summons. In effect, though, as it seems to me, the point you make is hardly material. Quite aside from any conceivable motive actuating the master-at-arms, and irrespective of the provocation to the blow, a martial court must needs in the present case confine its attention to the blow's consequence, which consequence justly is to be deemed not otherwise than as the striker's deed."

This utterance the full significance of which it was not at all likely that Billy took in, nevertheless caused him to turn a wistful interrogative look toward the speaker, a look in its dumb expressiveness not unlike that which a dog of generous breed might turn upon his master seeking in his face some elucidation of a precious gesture ambiguous to the canine intelligence. Nor was the same utterance without marked effect upon the three officers, more especially the soldier. Couched in it seemed to them a meaning unanticipated, involving a prejudgment on the speaker's part. It served to augment a mental disturbance previously evident enough.

The soldier once more spoke; in a tone of suggestive dubiety addressing at once his associates and Captain Vere: "Nobody is present—none of the ship's company, I mean, who might shed lateral light, if any is to be had, upon what remains mysterious in this matter."

"That is thoughtfully put," said Captain Vere. "I see your drift. Ay, there is a mystery; but, to use a Scriptural phrase, it is 'a mystery of iniquity,' a matter for psychologic theologians to discuss. But what has a military court to do with it? Not to add that for us any possible investigation of it is cut off by the lasting tongue-tie of—him—in yonder," again designating the mortuary stateroom. "The prisoner's deed,—with that alone we have to do."

To this, and particularly the closing reiteration, the marine soldier knowing not how aptly to reply, sadly abstained from saying aught. The first lieutenant who at the outset had not unnaturally assumed primacy in the court, now overwhelmingly instructed by a glance from Captain Vere, a glance more effective than words, resumed that primacy. Turning to the prisoner, "Budd," he said, and scarce in equable tones, "Budd, if you have aught further to say for yourself, say it now."

Upon this the young sailor turned another quick glance toward Captain Vere; then, as taking a hint from that aspect, a hint confirming his own instinct that silence was now best, replied to the lieutenant "I have said all, sir."

The marine—the same who had been the sentinel without the cabin door at the time that the foretopman followed by the master-at-arms, entered it—he, standing by the sailor throughout these judicial proceedings, was now directed to take him back to the after compartment originally assigned to the prisoner and his custodian. As the twain disappeared from view, the three officers as partially liberated from some inward constraint associated with Billy's mere presence, simultaneously stirred in their seats. They exchanged looks of troubled indecision, yet feeling that decide they must and without long delay. As for Captain Vere, he for the time stood unconsciously with his back toward them, apparently in one of his absent fits, gazing out from a sashed porthole to windward upon the monotonous blank of the twilight sea. But the court's silence continuing, broken only at moments by brief consultations in low earnest tones, this seemed to arm him and energize him. Turning, he to-and-fro paced the cabin athwart; in the returning ascent to windward, climbing the slant deck in the ship's lee roll; without knowing it symbolizing thus in his action a mind resolute to surmount difficulties even if against primitive instincts strong as the wind and the sea. Presently he came to a stand before the three. After scanning their faces he stood less as mustering his thoughts for expression, than as one inly deliberating how best to put them to well-meaning men not intellectually mature, men with whom it was necessary to demonstrate certain principles that were axioms to himself. Similar impatience as to talking is perhaps one reason that deters some minds from addressing any popular assemblies.

When speak he did, something both in the substance of what he said and his manner of saying it showed the influence of unshared studies modifying and tempering the practical training of an active career. This, along with his phraseology now and then was suggestive of the grounds whereon rested that imputation of a certain pedantry socially alleged against him by certain naval men of wholly practical cast, captains who nevertheless would frankly concede that His Majesty's navy mustered no more efficient officer of their grade than Starry Vere.

What he said was to this effect: "Hitherto I have been but the witness, little more; and I should hardly think now to take another tone, that of your coadjutor, for the time, did I not perceive in you,—at the crisis too—a troubled hesitancy, proceeding, I doubt not from the clash of military duty with moral scruple—scruple vitalized by compassion. For the compassion how can I otherwise than share it. But, mindful of paramount obligations I strive against scruples that may tend to enervate decision. Not, gentlemen, that I hide from myself that the case is an exceptional one. Speculatively regarded, it well might be referred to a jury of casuists. But for us here acting not as casuists or moralists, it is a case practical, and under martial law practically to be dealt with.

"But your scruples: do they move as in a dusk? Challenge them. Make them advance and declare themselves. Come now: do they import something like this: If, mindless of palliating circumstances, we are bound to regard the death of the master-at-arms as the prisoner's deed, then does that deed constitute a capital crime whereof the penalty is a mortal one. But in natural justice is nothing but the prisoner's overt act to be considered? How can we adjudge to summary and shameful death a fellow-creature innocent before God, and whom we feel to be so?—Does that state it aright? You sign sad assent. Well, I too feel that, the full force of that. It is Nature. But do these buttons that we wear attest that our allegiance is to Nature? No, to the King. Though the ocean, which is inviolate Nature primeval, though this be the element where we move and have our being as sailors, yet as the King's officers lies our duty in a sphere correspondingly natural? So little is that true, that in receiving our commissions we in the most important regards ceased to be natural free agents. When war is declared are we the commissioned fighters previously consulted? We fight at command. If our judgments approve the war, that is but coincidence. So in other particulars. So now. For suppose condemnation to follow these present proceedings. Would it be so much we ourselves that would condemn as it would be martial law operating through us? For that law and the rigor of it, we are not responsible. Our vowed responsibilty is in this: that however pitilessly that law may operate, we nevertheless adhere to it and administer it.

"But the exceptional in the matter moves the hearts within you. Even so too is mine moved. But let not warm hearts betray heads that should be cool. Ashore in a criminal case will an upright judge allow himself off the bench to be waylaid by some tender kinswoman of the accused seeking to touch him with her tearful plea? Well the heart here denotes the feminine in man is as that piteous woman, and hard though it be, she must here be ruled out."

He paused, earnestly studying them for a moment; then resumed.

"But something in your aspect seems to urge that it is not solely the heart that moves in you, but also the conscience, the private conscience. But tell me whether or not, occupying the position we do, private conscience should not yield to that imperial one formulated in the code under which alone we officially proceed?"

Here the three men moved in their seats, less convinced

than agitated by the course of an argument troubling but the more the spontaneous conflict within.

Perceiving which, the speaker paused for a moment; then abruptly changing his tone, went on.

"To steady us a bit, let us recur to the facts.—In wartime at sea a man-of-war's-man strikes his superior in grade, and the blow kills. Apart from its effect the blow itself is, according to the Articles of War, capital crime. Furthermore—"

"Ay, sir," emotionally broke in the officer of marines, "in one sense it was. But surely Budd purposed neither mutiny nor homicide."

"Surely not, my good man. And before a court less arbitrary and more merciful than a martial one, that plea would largely extenuate. At the Last Assizes[6] it shall acquit. But how here? We proceed under the law of the Mutiny Act. In feature no child can resemble his father more than that Act resembles in spirit the thing from which it derives—War. In His Majesty's service—in this ship indeed—there are Englishmen forced to fight for the King against their will. Against their conscience, for aught we know. Though as their fellow-creatures some of us may appreciate their position, yet as navy officers, what reck we of it? Still less recks the enemy. Our impressed men he would fain cut down in the same swath with our volunteers. As regards the enemy's naval conscripts, some of whom may even share our own abhorrence of the regicidal French Directory,[7] it is the same on our side. War looks but to the frontage, the appearance. And the Mutiny Act, War's child, takes after the father. Budd's intent or nonintent is nothing to the purpose.

"But while, put to it by those anxieties in you which I can not but respect, I only repeat myself—while thus strangely we prolong proceedings that should be summary—the enemy

---

6 Assizes are the highest judicial courts of review of the British counties; here the term refers to the scriptural Judgment Day.

7 The executive council of the French First Republic (1795-1799). This was the enemy against whom the British fleet was engaged in 1797, the year of this story (*cf.* the Preface).

may be sighted and an engagement result. We must do; and one of two things must we do—condemn or let go."

"Can we not convict and yet mitigate the penalty?" asked the junior lieutenant here speaking, and falteringly, for the first.

"Lieutenant, were that clearly lawful for us under the circumstances consider the consequences of such clemency. The people" (meaning the ship's company) "have native-sense; most of them are familiar with our naval usage and traditions; and how would they take it? Even could you explain to them —which our official position forbids—they, long molded by arbitrary discipline have not that kind of intelligent responsiveness that might qualify them to comprehend and discriminate. No, to the people the foretopman's deed however it be worded in the announcement will be plain homicide committed in a flagrant act of mutiny. What penalty for that should follow, they know. But it does not follow. *Why?* they will ruminate. You know what sailors are. Will they not revert to the recent outbreak at the Nore? Ay. They know the well-founded alarm—the panic it struck throughout England. Your clement sentence they would account pusillanimous. They would think that we flinch, that we are afraid of them—afraid of practising a lawful rigor singularly demanded at this juncture lest it should provoke new troubles. What shame to us such a conjecture on their part, and how deadly to discipline. You see then, whither prompted by duty and the law I steadfastly drive. But I beseech you, my friends, do not take me amiss. I feel as you do for this unfortunate boy. But did he know our hearts, I take him to be of that generous nature that he would feel even for us on whom in this military necessity so heavy a compulsion is laid."

With that, crossing the deck he resumed his place by the sashed porthole, tacitly leaving the three to come to a decision. On the cabin's opposite side the troubled court sat silent. Loyal lieges, plain and practical, though at bottom they dissented from some points Captain Vere had put to them, they were without the faculty, hardly had the inclination to gainsay one whom they felt to be an earnest man, one too not less their superior in mind than in naval rank. But it is not improbable that even such of his words as were not without influence over them, less came home to them than his closing appeal to their instinct as sea officers in the forethought he threw out as to the practical consequences to discipline, considering the unconfirmed tone of the fleet at the time, should a man-of-war's-man's violent killing at sea of a superior in grade be allowed to pass for aught else than a capital crime demanding prompt infliction of the penalty.

Not unlikely they were brought to something more or less akin to that harassed frame of mind which in the year 1842 actuated the commander of the U.S. brig-of-war *Somers* to resolve, under the so-called Articles of War, Articles modeled upon the English Mutiny Act, to resolve upon the execution at sea of a midshipman and two petty-officers as mutineers designing the seizure of the brig. Which resolution was carried out though in a time of peace and within not many days sail of home. An act vindicated by a naval court of inquiry subsequently convened ashore. History, and here cited without comment. True, the circumstances on board the *Somers* were different from those on board the *Indomitable*. But the urgency felt, well-warranted or otherwise, was much the same.

Says a writer whom few know, "Forty years after a battle it is easy for a noncombatant to reason about how it ought to have been fought. It is another thing personally and under fire to direct the fighting while involved in the obscuring smoke of it. Much so with respect to other emergencies involving considerations both practical and moral, and when it is imperative promptly to act. The greater the fog the more it imperils the steamer, and speed is put on though at the hazard of running somebody down. Little ween the snug card players in the cabin of the responsibilities of the sleepless man on the bridge."

In brief, Billy Budd was formally convicted and sentenced to be hung at the yardarm in the early morning watch, it being now night. Otherwise, as is customary in such cases, the sentence would forthwith have been carried out. In wartime on the field or in the fleet, a mortal punishment decreed by a drum-head court—on the field sometimes decreed by but a nod from the general—follows without delay on the heel of conviction without appeal.

XXIII

IT WAS CAPTAIN VERE himself who of his own motion communicated the finding of the court to the prisoner; for that purpose going to the compartment where he was in custody and bidding the marine there to withdraw for the time.

Beyond the communication of the sentence what took place at this interview was never known. But in view of the character of the twain briefly closeted in that stateroom, each radically sharing in the rarer qualities of our nature—so rare indeed as to be all but incredible to average minds however much cultivated—some conjectures may be ventured.

It would have been in consonance with the spirit of Captain Vere should he on this occasion have concealed nothing from the condemned one—should he indeed have frankly disclosed to him the part he himself had played in bringing about the decision, at the same time revealing his actuating motives. On Billy's side it is not improbable that such a confession would have been received in much the same spirit that prompted it. Not without a sort of joy indeed he might have appreciated the brave opinion of him implied in his captain making such a confidant of him. Nor, as to the sentence itself could he have been insensible that it was imparted to him as to one not afraid to die. Even more may have been. Captain Vere in the end may have developed the passion sometimes latent under an exterior stoical or indifferent. He was old enough to have been Billy's father. The austere devotee of military duty letting himself melt back into what remains primeval in our formalized humanity may in the end have caught Billy to his heart even as Abraham may have caught young Isaac on the brink of resolutely offering him up in obedience to the exacting behest. But there is no telling the sacrament, seldom if in any case revealed to the gadding world wherever under circumstances at all akin to those here attempted to be set forth two of great Nature's nobler order embrace. There is privacy at the time, inviolable to the survivor, and holy oblivion the sequel to each diviner magnanimity, providentially covers all at last.

The first to encounter Captain Vere in act of leaving the compartment was the senior lieutenant. The face he beheld, for the moment one expressive of the agony of the strong, was to that officer, though a man of fifty, a startling revelation. That the condemned one suffered less than he who mainly had effected the condemnation was apparently indicated by the former's exclamation in the scene soon perforce to be touched upon.

XXIV

OF A SERIES of incidents within a brief term rapidly following each other, the adequate narration may take up a term less brief, especially if explanation or comment here and there seem requisite to the better understanding of such incidents. Between the entrance into the cabin of him who never left it alive, and him who when he did leave it left it as one condemned to die; between this and the closeted interview just given less than an hour and a half had elapsed. It was an interval long enough however to awaken speculation among no few of the ship's company as to what it was that could be detaining in the cabin the master-at-arms and the sailor; for a rumor that both of them had been seen to enter it and neither of them had been seen to emerge, this rumor had got abroad upon the gundecks and in the tops; the people of a great warship being in one respect like villagers taking microscopic note of every outward movement or nonmovement going on. When therefore in weather not at all tempestuous all hands were called in the second dogwatch, a summons under such circumstances not usual in those hours, the crew were not wholly unprepared for some announcement extraordinary, one having connection too with the continued absence of the two men from their wonted haunts.

There was a moderate sea at the time; and the moon, newly risen and near to being at its full, silvered the white spardeck wherever not blotted by the clear-cut shadows horizontally thrown of fixtures and moving men. On either side the quarterdeck the marine guard under arms was drawn up; and Captain Vere standing in his place surrounded by all the wardroom officers, addressed his men. In so doing his manner showed neither more nor less than that property pertaining to his supreme position aboard his own ship. In clear terms and concise he told them what had taken place in the cabin; that the master-at-arms was dead; that he who had killed him had been already tried by a summary court and condemned to death; and that the execution would take place in the early morning watch. The word *mutiny* was not named in what he said. He refrained too from making the occasion an opportunity for any preachment as to the maintenance of discipline, thinking perhaps that under existing circumstances in the navy the consequence of violating discipline should be made to speak for itself.

Their captain's announcement was listened to by the throng of standing sailors in a dumbness like that of a seated congregation of believers in hell listening to the clergyman's announcement of his Calvinistic text.

At the close, however, a confused murmur went up. It began to wax. All but instantly, then, at a sign, it was pierced and suppressed by shrill whistles of the boatswain and his mates piping down one watch.

To be prepared for burial Claggart's body was delivered to certain petty-officers of his mess. And here, not to clog the sequel with lateral matters, it may be added that at a suitable hour, the master-at-arms was committed to the sea with every funeral honor properly belonging to his naval grade.

In this proceeding as in every public one growing out of the tragedy strict adherence to usage was observed. Nor in any point could it have been at all deviated from, either with respect to Claggart or Billy Budd, without begetting undesirable speculations in the ship's company, sailors, and more particularly men-of-war's men, being of all men the greatest sticklers for usage.

For similar cause, all communication between Captain Vere and the condemned one ended with the closeted interview already given, the latter being now surrendered to the ordinary routine preliminary to the end. This transfer under guard from the captain's quarters was effected without unusual precautions—at least no visible ones.

If possible not to let the men so much as surmise that their officers anticipate aught amiss from them is the tacit rule in a military ship. And the more that some sort of trouble should really be apprehended the more do the officers keep that apprehension to themselves; though not the less unostentatious vigilance may be augmented.

In the present instance the sentry placed over the prisoner had strict orders to let no one have communication with him but the chaplain. And certain unobtrusive measures were taken absolutely to insure this point.

XXV

IN A SEVENTY-FOUR of the old order the deck known as the upper gundeck was the one covered over by the spardeck which last though not without its armament was for the most part exposed to the weather. In general it was at all hours free from hammocks; those of the crew swinging on the lower gundeck, and berthdeck, the latter being not only a dormitory but also the place for the stowing of the sailors' bags, and on both sides lined with the large chests or movable pantries of the many messes of the men.

On the starboard side of the *Indomitable's* upper gundeck,

behold Billy Budd under sentry lying prone in irons in one of
the bays formed by the regular spacing of the guns comprising the batteries on either side. All these pieces were of the
heavier caliber of that period. Mounted on lumbering wooden
carriages they were hampered with cumbersome harness of
breeching and strong side-tackles for running them out. Guns
and carriages, together with the long rammers and shorter
lintstocks lodged in loops overhead—all these, as customary,
were painted black; and the heavy hempen breechings tarred
to the same tint, wore the like livery of the undertakers. In
contrast with the funereal hue of these surroundings the prone
sailor's exterior apparel, white jumper and white duck trousers, each more or less soiled, dimly glimmered in the obscure
light of the bay like a patch of discolored snow in early
April lingering at some upland cave's black mouth. In effect
he is already in his shroud or the garments that shall serve
him in lieu of one. Over him but scarce illuminating him, two
battle lanterns swing from two massive beams of the deck
above. Fed with the oil supplied by the war-contractors
(whose gains, honest or otherwise, are in every land an
anticipated portion of the harvest of death) with flickering
splashes of dirty yellow light they pollute the pale moonshine,
all but ineffectually struggling in obstructed flecks through
the open ports from which the tompioned[8] cannon protrude.
Other lanterns at intervals serve but to bring out somewhat the
obscurer bays which like small confessionals or side-chapels
in a cathedral branch from the long dim-vistaed broad aisle
between the two batteries of that covered tier.

Such was the deck where now lay the Handsome Sailor.
Through the rose-tan of his complexion, no pallor could have
shown. It would have taken days of sequestration from the
winds and the sun to have brought about the effacement of
that. But the skeleton in the cheekbone at the point of its
angle was just beginning delicately to be defined under the
warm-tinted skin. In fervid hearts self-contained some brief

_____
8 Usually, "tampioned"; plugged with a tampion, as the muzzle of a gun
not in use.

experiences devour our human tissue as secret fire in a ship's hold consumes cotton in the bale.

But now lying between the two guns, as nipped in the vice of fate, Billy's agony, mainly proceeding from a generous young heart's virgin experience of the diabolical incarnate and effective in some men—the tension of that agony was over now. It survived not the something healing in the closeted interview with Captain Vere. Without movement, he lay as in a trance. That adolescent expression previously noted as his, taking on something akin to the look of a slumbering child in the cradle when the warm hearth-glow of the still chamber at night plays on the dimples that at whiles mysteriously form in the cheek, silently coming and going there. For now and then in the gyved one's trance a serene happy light born of some wandering reminiscence or dream would diffuse itself over his face, and then wane away only anew to return.

The chaplain coming to see him and finding him thus, and perceiving no sign that he was conscious of his presence, attentively regarded him for a space, then slipping aside, withdrew for the time, peradventure feeling that even he the minister of Christ though receiving his stipend from Mars had no consolation to proffer which could result in a peace transcending that which he beheld. But in the small hours he came again. And the prisoner now awake to his surroundings noticed his approach and civilly, all but cheerfully, welcomed him. But it was to little purpose that in the interview following the good man sought to bring Billy Budd to some godly understanding that he must die, and at dawn. True, Billy himself freely referred to his death as a thing close at hand; but it was something in the way that children will refer to death in general, who yet among their other sports will play a funeral with hearse and mourners.

Not that like children Billy was incapable of conceiving what death really is. No, but he was wholly without irrational fear of it, a fear more prevalent in highly civilized communities than those so-called barbarous ones which in all respects stand nearer to unadulterate Nature. And, as elsewhere said, a barbarian Billy radically was; as much so, for all the costume, as his countrymen the British captives, living trophies, made to march in the Roman triumph of Germanicus.[9] Quite as much so as those later barbarians, young men probably, and picked specimens among the earlier British converts to Christianity, at least nominally such and taken to Rome (as today converts from lesser isles of the sea may be taken to London) of whom the Pope of that time, admiring the strangeness of their personal beauty so unlike the Italian stamp, their clear ruddy complexion and curled flaxen locks, exclaimed, "Angles" (meaning *English* the modern derivative) "Angles do you call them? And is it because they look so like angels?" Had it been later in time one would think that the Pope had in mind Fra Angelico's[1] seraphs some of whom, plucking apples in gardens of the Hesperides have the faint rose-bud complexion of the more beautiful English girls.

If in vain the good chaplain sought to impress the young barbarian with ideas of death akin to those conveyed in the skull, dial, and crossbones on old tombstones; equally futile to all appearance were his efforts to bring home to him the thought of salvation and a Saviour. Billy listened, but less out of awe or reverence perhaps than from a certain natural politeness; doubtless at bottom regarding all that in much the same way that most mariners of his class take any discourse abstract or out of the common tone of the work-a-day world. And this sailor way of taking clerical discourse is not wholly unlike the way in which the pioneer of Christianity full of transcendent miracles was received long ago on tropic isles by any superior *savage* so called—a Tahitian, say of Captain Cook's time or shortly after that time.[2] Out of natural courtesy he received, but did not appropriate. It was like a

---

9 Germanicus Caesar (15 B.C.–19 A.D.), Roman general and conqueror, whose triumphs were spectacularly celebrated in Rome in 17 A.D.

1 Italian friar-painter of the fifteenth century, famous for his religious frescoes. The Hesperides, in classical myth, were fabulous gardens where grew golden apples, guarded by a dragon.

2 Captain James Cook (1728–1779), British explorer, made remarkable discoveries in the Pacific, visiting the Marquesas Islands and Tahiti, where Melville adventured in 1842.

gift placed in the palm of an outreached hand upon which the fingers do not close.

But the *Indomitable's* chaplain was a discreet man possessing the good sense of a good heart. So he insisted not in his vocation here. At the instance of Captain Vere, a lieutenant had apprised him of pretty much everything as to Billy; and since he felt that innocence was even a better thing than religion wherewith to go to judgment, he reluctantly withdrew; but in his emotion not without first performing an act strange enough in an Englishman, and under the circumstances yet more so in any regular priest. Stooping over, he kissed on the fair cheek his fellowman, a felon in martial law, one who though on the confines of death he felt he could never convert to a dogma; nor for all that did he fear for his future.

Marvel not that having been made acquainted with the young sailor's essential innocence (an irruption of heretic thought hard to suppress) the worthy man lifted not a finger to avert the doom of such a martyr to martial discipline. So to do would not only have been as idle as invoking the desert, but would also have been an audacious transgression of the bounds of his function, one as exactly prescribed to him by military law as that of the boatswain or any other naval officer. Bluntly put, a chaplain is the minister of the Prince of Peace serving in the host of the god of war—Mars. As such, he is as incongruous as that musket of Blücher etc.[3] at Christmas. Why then is he there? Because he indirectly subserves the purpose attested by the cannon; because, too, he lends the sanction of the religion of the meek to that which practically is the abrogation of everything but brute force.

---

3 The manuscript is illegible; "Blücher etc." is a conjectural reading. Prussian Field Marshal Gebhard von Blücher (1742–1819), who had aided Wellington at Waterloo, was still famous.

XXVI

THE NIGHT SO LUMINOUS on the spardeck but otherwise on the cavernous ones below, levels so like the tiered galleries in a coalmine—the luminous night passed away. But, like the prophet in the chariot disappearing in heaven and dropping his mantle to Elisha, the withdrawing night transferred its pale robe to the breaking day. A meek shy light appeared in the East, where stretched a diaphanous fleece of white furrowed vapor. That light slowly waxed. Suddenly eight bells was struck aft, responded to by one louder metallic stroke from forward. It was four o'clock in the morning. Instantly the silver whistles were heard summoning all hands to witness punishment. Up through the great hatchways rimmed with racks of heavy shot, the watch below came pouring overspreading with the watch already on deck the space between the mainmast and foremast including that occupied by the capacious launch and the black booms tiered on either side of it, boat and booms making a summit of observation for the powder boys and younger tars. A different group comprising one watch of topmen leaned over the rail of that sea balcony, no small one in a seventy-four, looking down on the crowd below. Man or boy none spake but in whisper, and few spake at all. Captain Vere—as before, the central figure among the assembled commissioned officers—stood nigh the break of the poopdeck facing forward. Just below him on the quarterdeck the marines in full equipment were drawn up much as at the scene of the promulgated sentence.

At sea in the old time, the execution by halter of a military sailor was generally from the foreyard. In the present instance, for special reasons the mainyard was assigned. Under an arm of that lee yard[4] the prisoner was presently brought

---

4 Melville wrote both "weather" and "lee" above the word "yard," and failed to cancel either of these opposites. The lee yard would be more likely, as being more sheltered.

up, the chaplain attending him. It was noted at the time and remarked upon afterwards that in this final scene the good man evinced little or nothing of the perfunctory. Brief speech indeed he had with the condemned one, but the genuine Gospel was less on his tongue than in his aspect and manner toward him. The final preparations personal to the latter being speedily brought to an end by two boatswain's-mates, the consummation impended. Billy stood facing aft. At the penultimate moment, his words, his only ones, words wholly unobstructed in the utterance were these—"God bless Captain Vere!" Syllables so unanticipated coming from one with the ignominious hemp about his neck—a conventional felon's benediction directed aft towards the quarters of honor; syllables too delivered in the clear melody of a singing bird on the point of launching from the twig, had a phenomenal effect, not unenhanced by the rare personal beauty of the young sailor spiritualized now through late experiences so poignantly profound.

Without volition as it were, as if indeed the ship's populace were but the vehicles of some vocal current electric, with one voice from alow and aloft came a resonant sympathetic echo —"God bless Captain Vere!" And yet at that instant Billy alone must have been in their hearts, even as he was in their eyes.

At the pronounced words and the spontaneous echo that voluminously rebounded them, Captain Vere, either through stoic self-control or a sort of momentary paralysis induced by emotional shock, stood erectly rigid as a musket in the ship armorer's rack.

The hull deliberately recovering from the periodic roll to leeward was just regaining an even keel, when the last signal, a preconcerted dumb one, was given. At the same moment it chanced that the vapory fleece hanging low in the East, was shot through with a soft glory as of the fleece of the Lamb of God seen in mystical vision, and simultaneously therewith, watched by the wedged mass of upturned faces, Billy ascended; and, ascending, took the full rose of the dawn.

In the pinioned figure, arrived at the yard end, to the wonder of all no motion was apparent, none save that created by the ship's motion, in moderate weather so majestic in a great ship ponderously cannoned.

XXVII

A digression

WHEN SOME DAYS afterward in reference to the singularity just mentioned, the purser, a rather ruddy rotund person more accurate as an accountant than profound as a philosopher, said at mess to the surgeon, "What testimony to the force lodged in willpower," the latter—saturnine spare and tall, one in whom a discreet causticity went along with a manner less genial than polite, replied, "Your pardon, Mr. Purser. In a hanging scientifically conducted—and under special orders I myself directed how Budd's was to be effected —any movement following the completed suspension and originating in the body suspended, such movement indicates mechanical spasm in the muscular system. Hence the absence of that is no more attributable to willpower as you call it than to horsepower—begging your pardon."

"But this muscular spasm you speak of, is not that in a degree more or less invariable in these cases?"

"Assuredly so, Mr. Purser."

"How then, my good sir, do you account for its absence in this instance?"

"Mr. Purser, it is clear that your sense of the singularity in this matter equals not mine. You account for it by what you call willpower a term not yet included in the lexicon of science. For me I do not, with my present knowledge pretend to account for it at all. Even should we assume the hypothesis that at the first touch of the halyards the action of Budd's heart, intensified by extraordinary emotion at its climax, abruptly stopped—much like a watch when in care-lessly winding it up you strain at the finish, thus snapping the chain—even under that hypothesis how account for the phenomenon that followed?"

"You admit then that the absence of spasmodic movement was phenomenal."

"It was phenomenal, Mr. Purser, in the sense that it was an appearance the cause of which is not immediately to be assigned."

"But tell me, my dear sir," pertinaciously continued the other, "was the man's death effected by the halter, or was it a species of euthanasia?"

"*Euthanasia,* Mr. Purser, is something like your *willpower:* I doubt its authenticity as a scientific term—begging your pardon again. It is at once imaginative and metaphysical—in short, Greek. But," abruptly changing his tone, "there is a case in the sick bay that I do not care to leave to my assistants. Beg your pardon, but excuse me." And rising from the mess he formally withdrew.

XXVIII

THE SILENCE AT THE moment of execution and for a moment or two continuing thereafter, a silence but emphasized by the regular wash of the sea against the hull or the flutter of a sail caused by the helmsman's eyes being tempted astray, this emphasized silence was gradually disturbed by a sound not easily to be verbally rendered. Whoever has heard the freshet-wave of a torrent suddenly swelled by pouring showers in tropical mountains, showers not shared by the plain; who-ever has heard the first muffled murmur of its sloping advance through precipitous woods, may form some conception of the sound now heard. The seeming remoteness of its source was because of its murmurous indistinctness since it came from close-by, even from the men massed on the ship's open deck. Being inarticulate, it was dubious in significance further than it seemed to indicate some capricious revulsion of thought or feeling such as mobs ashore are liable to, in the present instance possibly implying a sullen revocation on the men's part of their involuntary echoing of Billy's benediction. But ere the murmur had time to wax into clamor it was met by a strategic command, the more telling that it came with abrupt unexpectedness.

"Pipe down the starboard watch, Boatswain, and see that they go."

Shrill as the shriek of the sea hawk the whistles of the boatswain and his mates pierced that ominous low sound, dissipating it; and yielding to the mechanism of discipline the throng was thinned by one half. For the remainder most of them were set to temporary employments connected with trimming the yards and so forth, business readily to be got up to serve occasion by any officer-of-the-deck.

Now each proceeding that follows a mortal sentence pronounced at sea by a drum-head court is characterised by promptitude not perceptibly merging into hurry, though bordering that. The hammock, the one which had been Billy's bed when alive, having already been ballasted with shot and otherwise prepared to serve for his canvas coffin, the last offices of the sea undertakers, the sailmaker's mates, were now speedily completed. When everything was in readiness a second call for all hands made necessary by the strategic movement before mentioned was sounded and now to witness burial.

The details of this closing formality it needs not to give. But when the tilted plank let slide its freight into the sea, a second strange human murmur was heard, blended now with another inarticulate sound proceeding from certain larger sea fowl whose attention having been attracted by the peculiar commotion in the water resulting from the heavy sloped dive of the shotted hammock into the sea, flew screaming to the spot. So near the hull did they come, that the stridor or bony creak of their gaunt double-jointed pinions was audible. As the ship under light airs passed on, leaving the burial spot astern, they still kept circling it low down with the moving shadow of their outstretched wings and the croaked requiem of their cries.

Upon sailors as superstitious as those of the age preceding ours, men-of-war's men too who had just beheld the prodigy of repose in the form suspended in air and now foundering in the deeps; to such mariners the action of the sea fowl though dictated by mere animal greed for prey, was big with no prosaic significance. An uncertain movement began among them, in which some encroachment was made. It was tolerated but for a moment. For suddenly the drumbeat to quarters, which familiar sound happening at least twice every day, had upon the present occasion a signal peremptoriness in it. True martial discipline long continued superinduces in average man a sort of impulse of docility whose operation at the official sound of command much resembles in its promptitude the effect of an instinct.

The drumbeat dissolved the multitude, distributing most of them along the batteries of the two covered gundecks. There, as wont, the guns' crews stood by their respective cannon erect and silent. In due course the first officer, sword under arm and standing in his place on the quarterdeck, formally received the successive reports of the sworded lieutenants commanding the sections of batteries below; the last of which reports being made, the summed report he delivered with the customary salute to the commander. All this occupied time, which in the present case, was the object of beating to quarters at an hour prior to the customary one. That such variance from usage was authorized by an officer like Captain Vere, a martinet as some deemed him, was evidence of the necessity for unusual action implied in what he deemed to be temporarily the mood of his men. "With mankind," he would say, "forms, measured forms are everything; and that is the import couched in the story of Orpheus with his lyre spellbinding the wild denizens of the wood." And this he once applied to the disruption of forms going on across the Channel and the consequences thereof.

At this unwonted muster at quarters, all proceeded as at the regular hour. The band on the quarterdeck played a sacred air. After which the chaplain went through the customary morning service. That done, the drum beat the retreat, and toned by music and religious rites subserving the discipline and purpose of war, the men in their wonted orderly manner, dispersed to the places allotted them when not at the guns.

And now it was full day. The fleece of low-hanging vapor had vanished, licked up by the sun that late had so glorified it. And the circumambient air in the clearness of its serenity was like smooth white marble in the polished block not yet removed from the marble-dealer's yard.

XXIX

THE SYMMETRY OF form attainable in pure fiction can not so readily be achieved in a narration essentially having less to do with fable than with fact. Truth uncompromisingly told will always have its ragged edges; hence the conclusion of such a narration is apt to be less finished than an architectural finial.

How it fared with the Handsome Sailor during the year of the Great Mutiny has been faithfully given. But though properly the story ends with his life, something in way of sequel will not be amiss. Three brief chapters will suffice.

In the general re-christening under the Directory of the craft originally forming the navy of the French monarchy, the *St. Louis* line-of-battle ship was named the *Athéiste*. Such a name, like some other substituted ones in the Revolutionary fleet while proclaiming the infidel audacity of the ruling power was yet, though not so intended to be, the aptest name, if one consider it, ever given to a warship; far more so indeed than the *Devastation*, the *Erebus* (the *Hell*) and similar names bestowed upon fighting ships.

On the return passage to the English fleet from the de- tached cruise during which occurred the events already recorded, the *Indomitable* fell in with the *Athéiste*. An engagement ensued; during which Captain Vere in the act of putting his ship alongside the enemy with a view of throwing his boarders across her bulwarks, was hit by a musketball from a porthole of the enemy's main cabin. More than disabled he dropped to the deck and was carried below to the same cockpit where some of his men already lay. The senior lieutenant took command. Under him the enemy was finally captured and though much crippled was by rare good fortune successfully taken into Gibraltar, an English port not very distant from the scene of the fight. There, Captain Vere with the rest of the wounded was put ashore. He lingered for some days, but the end came. Unhappily he was cut off too early for the Nile and Trafalgar.[5] The spirit that spite its philosophic austerity may yet have indulged in the most secret of all passions, ambition, never attained to the fullness of fame.

Not long before death while lying under the influence of that magical drug which soothing the physical frame mysteriously operates on the subtler element in man, he was heard to murmur words inexplicable to his attendant—"Billy Budd, Billy Budd." That these were not the accents of remorse, would seem clear from what the attendant said to the *Indomitable's* senior officer of marines who, as the most reluctant to condemn of the members of the drum-head court, too well knew, though here he kept the knowledge to himself, who Billy Budd was.

XXX

SOME FEW WEEKS after the execution, among other matters under the head of *News from the Mediterranean*, there appeared in a naval chronicle of the time, an authorized weekly publication, an account of the affair. It was doubtless for the

---

5 Admiral Nelson destroyed Napoleon's fleet at the Battle of the Nile (1798); at Trafalgar in 1805 he ended the French naval wars with victory, and was himself killed.

most part written in good faith, though the medium, partly rumor, through which the facts must have reached the writer, served to deflect and in part falsify them. The account was as follows:

"On the tenth of the last month a deplorable occurrence took place on board H.M.S. *Indomitable*. John Claggart, the ship's master-at-arms, discovering that some sort of plot was incipient among an inferior section of the ship's company, and that the ringleader was one William Budd; he, Claggart, in the act of arraigning the man before the captain was vindictively stabbed to the heart by the suddenly drawn sheath-knife of Budd.

"The deed and the implement employed, sufficiently suggest that though mustered into the service under an English name the assassin was no Englishman, but one of those aliens adopting English cognomens whom the present extraordinary necessities of the service have caused to be admitted into it in considerable numbers.

"The enormity of the crime and the extreme depravity of the criminal, appear the greater in view of the character of the victim, a middle-aged man respectable and discreet, belonging to that minor official grade, the petty-officers, upon whom, as none know better than the commissioned gentlemen, the efficiency of His Majesty's navy so largely depends. His function was a responsible one; at once onerous and thankless and his fidelity in it the greater because of his strong patriotic impulse. In this instance as in so many other instances in these days, the character of this unfortunate man signally refutes, if refutation were needed, that peevish saying attributed to the late Dr. Johnson, that patriotism is the last refuge of a scoundrel.

"The criminal paid the penalty of his crime. The promptitude of the punishment has proved salutary. Nothing amiss is now apprehended aboard H.M.S. *Indomitable*."

The above, appearing in a publication now long ago superannuated and forgotten, is all that hitherto has stood in human record to attest what manner of men respectively were John Claggart and Billy Budd.

XXXI

EVERYTHING IS FOR A term remarkable in navies. Any tangible object associated with some striking incident of the service is converted into a monument. The spar from which the foretopman was suspended, was for some few years kept trace of by the blue-jackets. Their knowledge followed it from ship to dockyard and again from dockyard to ship, still pursuing it even when at last reduced to a mere dockyard boom. To them a chip of it was as a piece of the cross. Ignorant though they were of the secret facts of the tragedy, and not thinking but that the penalty was somehow unavoidably inflicted from the naval point of view, for all that they instinctively felt that Billy was a sort of man as incapable of mutiny as of willful murder. They recalled the fresh young image of the Handsome Sailor, that face never deformed by a sneer or subtler vile freak of the heart within. Their impression of him was doubtless deepened by the fact that he was gone, and in a measure mysteriously gone. At the time on the gundecks of the *Indomitable* the general estimate of his nature and its unconscious simplicity eventually found rude utterance from another foretopman, one of his own watch; gifted, as some sailors are, with an artless poetic temperament; the tarry hands made some lines which after circulating among the shipboard crew for a while, finally got rudely printed at Portsmouth as a ballad. The title given to it was the sailor's.

Billy in the Darbies⁶

Good of the chaplain to enter Lone Bay
And down on his marrowbones here and pray
For the likes just o' me, Billy Budd.—But look:
Through the port comes the moonshine astray!

------

6 Manacles or irons.

It tips the guard's cutlas and silvers this nook;
But 'twill die in the dawning of Billy's last day.
A jewel block they'll make of me tomorrow,
Pendant pearl from the yardarm end
Like the eardrop I gave to Bristol Molly—
O, 'tis me, not the sentence they'll suspend.
Ay, Ay, all is up; and I must up too
Early in the morning, aloft from alow.
On an empty stomach, now, never it would do.
They'll give me a nibble—bit o' biscuit ere I go.
Sure, a messmate will reach me the last parting cup;
But, turning heads away from the hoist and the belay,
Heaven knows who will have the running of me up!
No pipe to those halyards.—But aren't it all sham?
A blur's in my eyes; it is dreaming that I am.
A hatchet to my hawser? all adrift to go?
The drum roll to grog, and Billy never know?
But Donald he has promised to stand by the plank;
So I'll shake a friendly hand ere I sink.
But—no! It is dead then I'll be, come to think.—
I remember Taff the Welshman when he sank.
And his cheek it was like the budding pink.
But me they'll lash me in hammock, drop me deep.
Fathoms down, fathoms down, how I'll dream fast asleep.
I feel it stealing now. Sentry, are you there?
Just ease this darbies at the wrist, and roll me over fair,
I am sleepy, and the oozy weeds about me twist.

April 19th, 1891

Classics That Will Delight Readers Of Every Age!